Promised to the Wolves

Devil Mountain Wolf Shifters: Book Six

A Paranormal Menage Romance

Jasmine Wylder

© Copyright 2020 by Pure Passion Reads - All rights reserved.
1. Edition

Title: Promised to the Wolves
ISBN: 9798656605199
Author: Jasmine Wylder
Publication Date: June 24, 2020
Publisher: Pure Passion Reads GmbH, Uferstr. 3a, 39307 Roßdorf

In no way is it legal to reproduce, duplicate, or transmit any part of this document in either electronic means or in printed format. Recording of this publication is strictly prohibited and any storage of this document is not allowed unless with written permission from the publisher. All rights reserved.

Respective publisher owns all copyrights not held by the author.

DEDICATION

To my loved ones B & B, who encouraged me to fly toward my dream:
Let's soar.

CONTENTS

Chapter One	8
Chapter Two	15
Chapter Three	23
Chapter Four	30
Chapter Five	37
Chapter Six	43
Chapter Seven	50
Chapter Eight	56
Chapter Nine	63
Chapter Ten	70
Chapter Eleven	77
Chapter Twelve	84
Chapter Thirteen	91
Chapter Fourteen	97
Chapter Fifteen	100
Chapter Sixteen	107
Chapter Seventeen	114
Chapter Eighteen	121

Chapter Nineteen	129
Epilogue	135
Thank You!	145
About the Author	146

CHAPTER ONE

Exhaustion weighed down Jamie's limbs with the stink of coffee, grease, and sweat overpowering her nose. Work had been hell. A double shift at the only diner in town—not to mention the only diner for miles around sitting on a major highway that saw a lot of traffic all through the day and night—was enough to make anybody a little bit crazy.

It didn't help that they were chronically understaffed and that the owner of the diner, Bill, had decided to come in today and yell at Jamie and the other wait staff about 'wasting money' by doing things like using the proper dosage of sanitizer to clean the dishes as per the law instead of halving it like he wanted them to.

Jamie tiptoed into the house, hoping that her stepfather wasn't awake yet. The sun was already in the mid-morning sky and there was a lot of work to be done around the farm if he wanted to get anything planted, but that didn't mean he'd be awake. He had been drinking the previous day when she left for work—and for once she had been glad to be leaving. She had only taken the job at the diner to have an excuse to get away from him. Normally she'd be going out and getting the fields tilled and ready for planting potatoes and corn. Life was getting to a point where it was unbearable to spend any time in the house at all. The only time she had any sense of calm was when she was working the land. But even that wasn't as much of an escape as it used to be. Not when she was exhausted all the time.

"Jamie, get in here," her stepfather called from the living room as she slipped off her shoes.

With a flinch, Jamie put her jacket up on the proper hook. So much for sneaking in. Quietly, she padded into the living room. Only to stop, her eyes widening, when she saw Shawn and Adrian, two of the wolf shifters of Devil Mountain, sitting on the couch that had belonged to her great-grandmother. A flush worked its way up her neck and cheeks.

Here she was, covered in diner grease and sweat, her makeup having rubbed off throughout a sixteen-hour workday, her feet aching, her hair wound flat against her skull to keep it out of the way and her father was calling her in to talk with him now? In front of the two sexiest, most eligible men in Deville? There weren't a lot of single men in the town or surrounding area and of those single men, there were none who had their own land *and* hadn't known her from high school.

Not to mention that these were two of the few people who knew that she was a wolf shifter herself. She claimed diabetes to cover the multiple injections of blockers she gave herself in a day to keep her wolf at bay, but most people assumed she was into drugs. It was something she was happy to let people keep thinking, honestly. She was already an outcast, the last thing she needed was yet another thing for them to see her as different.

She wrapped her arms around her waist as she looked uneasily at her stepfather, whose self-satisfied grin made her stomach clench. What was he up to? Slowly, she eased herself backward. If she whined enough about being tired would he let her at least rest before he sprang whatever trap he'd set for her?

"I have good news for you, Jamie," her stepfather said as his grin widened. "Something has happened that will be of great benefit to you."

What did he mean by that? He never did anything that was of benefit to her. The best she could hope for when it came to him was that whatever schemes he cooked up wouldn't hurt her too much. She eased another foot behind herself.

"Can it wait until later? I'm really tired and I smell like the diner. I really should get cleaned up and head to bed." Her voice trembled, but the men didn't seem to notice or care. At the mention of bed, however, Adrian and Shawn smirked at one another. It made Jamie feel all the worse. She liked these two, or at least thought she did, and didn't want to be reduced to the fatty hamburger ready to be consumed that so many of the guys in Deville seemed to think of her.

She had been born in Deville, lived on this farm her entire life. Somehow in her days of oversized sweaters and looking at her feet while she walked, the boys she grew up with decided that since she never went on dates—or rather since none of them asked her out—that meant she was starving for any scrap of masculine affection. None of them bothered to ask her to a dance or dinner or movie or anything like that. Instead, they'd tell her since all the hot girls were taken, they'd let her bend over for them.

As though she had any desire to do that. And then, when she refused, they started rumors that she did anyway. It only got worse when someone, she didn't know who, decided to tell everybody they met that she was sleeping with her stepfather. So here she was, the only slut in Deville who had never been so much as kissed.

"I have to go," she mumbled, spinning on her heel.

She hadn't even gotten halfway down the hallway before her stepfather caught up with her. He grabbed her arm tight enough to make her flinch and dragged her to her bedroom. Jamie glanced down the hallway, frightened about what the wolves would think about this, but they were nowhere in sight.

A duffel bag sat on her bed and her stepfather shoved it into her chest. "I've already packed for you. You're leaving with the wolves, Jamie. It's time you stopped living at home."

Jamie opened her mouth and closed it again, her eyes going wide. What was he talking about? She had tried, at times, to move out and rent her own place to get space from him. Every single time, he had ended up telling her to come back. Whether for money or work around the farm, it didn't matter. All he had to do was threaten to sell the land and she came back, doing whatever she needed to do to keep it.

This farm had been in her biological father's family for generations. He'd been orphaned in his teens and worked hard to keep the land he'd inherited. He'd died in a tractor accident when Jamie was only a year old. Her mother had remarried shortly after. Not because she loved Jamie's stepfather, far from it, but because she didn't want to lose the land and didn't know what to do with her life without a man around.

And then she'd died. Supposedly it had been an accident. She'd mixed up her pills and ended up falling asleep at the wheel and ended up in the river. Supposedly. But Jamie always thought that it was on purpose. That her mother couldn't take it anymore and left her alone. And the farm had gone to her mother's husband because Jamie wasn't yet an adult.

Now that she was an adult? He owned the property. And she had no means of fighting for the title. Every cent she earned went to paying taxes and upkeep. Because, of course, her stepfather refused to pay for it. She loved this land. Loved the connection it gave her to her ancestors. She couldn't let it go.

And now he was forcing her away?

"You're not selling, are you?" she asked anxiously, her hands starting to tremble as she clutched the duffel bag tighter.

"Selling *you*, you mean?" her stepfather grinned. "Nothing like that. There is no money trading hands. But I've decided it's time for you to leave and start being an actual adult. I can't keep carrying you forever. So, I've promised you to them. You'll be going with them, and you'll be their problem now."

"Promised?" Jamie's voice rose in pitch. What was he talking about?

Her stepfather rolled his eyes. "That's what you wolves do, isn't it? Give away your children. It's the only way you'll get a mate, anyway. You should be lucky that they want you with your hippo hips and double chin."

"But…" She wracked her brains, trying to figure out what had started this. "What did I do?"

Her stepfather rolled his eyes again. "Miranda doesn't like that you are still living with your stepfather when you're a grown woman."

So that was it. His new girlfriend didn't like the situation. Jamie swallowed hard. She had been polite to Miranda. Did the normal cooking, clean-up, everything while Miranda lazed around complaining about everything she did. Jamie had gone out of her way to help Miranda feel at home, knowing what people thought of her. But she supposed it wasn't enough.

Did Miranda know, she wondered, that all the household work would now be thrown on her? That she was going to be cooking and cleaning for her boyfriend? It hurt Jamie's heart to think of what the state of the farm would be once Miranda and her stepfather broke up and he dragged Jamie back.

But if he was giving her to Shawn and Adrian, would she even be able to come back? She bit her lip hard as tears filled her eyes. Had everything she had been working for gotten taken away from her? Was this the last time she was going to stand on her beloved farm? He had never done anything like this before.

"This farm should be mine," Jamie managed to gasp out. Her throat was swollen, and tears still threatened to fall, but she didn't know what to do. "If Miranda doesn't like me being around, maybe you should move in with her and transfer the property title to me like you've been saying you would since Mom died!"

Her stepfather glared at her coldly, any trace of gentleness having disappeared. "This land belongs to me, Jamie. You would have lost it long ago if I hadn't stepped in to manage it for you. Do you think that I'm just going to give it up for you to squander?"

"But I know how to run it. I do more work around here than—"

"Maybe I should just put it on the market right now, then." Her stepfather glowered at her, danger in his eyes. "Can you afford to buy it from me? If you want this farm, Jamie, then you are going to prove yourself a capable adult by doing what I tell you. Understood?"

Jamie's lip trembled, but she bit it and nodded. She pulled the duffel bag over her shoulder, trying not to break down. When she moved to her dresser to get the jewelry box that her mother had left her, though, her stepfather grabbed her arm and pushed her toward the door.

"Don't want to weigh you down with too many things now do we?" he hissed in her ear.

Her shoulders slumped, but she didn't have the strength to argue with him. She felt sick at heart, like there was no point to anything. The blockers that she had last used were starting to wear off and that unfamiliar sensation of her wolf made her shiver all the more. She never knew how to understand what it wanted from her. Now, it was pawing groggily at her ribs. She pushed it down as she was ushered from the house and into a large truck. Shawn and Adrian pressed in on her from either side as she clutched her duffel bag to her chest.

"This should be fun," Shawn said as he started the truck. "Consider this a thank you for helping take care of me when I was injured a few months back."

Thank you? Jamie pressed her face into her duffel bag. They were already taking her farm from her. What else would they steal from her as 'thanks'?

CHAPTER TWO

Adrian jumped from the truck as they stopped in front of Shawn's cabin. They had had quite a long discussion about where they were going to house their new Jamie. Having a woman around, well anybody, really, was going to be an adjustment.

They had considered putting her in Adrian's campground, in one of the nicer cabins there. But it wasn't exactly near any cabins where people actually lived. Adrian ran it on an honor system more than anything, with a number for people to call him if they needed something. Now wasn't the time of year for camping, anyway. The cabins didn't have any heat, nor did they have indoor plumbing or electricity. No, it was just better for her to live close to one of them.

In the end, they decided on Shawn's property because he still had the little hobbit-hole he'd lived in before building his cabin. From the shell-shocked look on Jamie's face as she stumbled from the truck, they had made the right choice. After all, both cabins only had one bedroom each, although Adrian supposed that the offices could have been refurbished into bedrooms.

He could only imagine how terrified she would be if she

was living in the cabin with them, however. This was happening all rather suddenly and even Adrian was a little uncertain of how it was going. He couldn't imagine how utterly stunned Jamie must be about all of this.

"Do you both live here?" Jamie asked, her voice small, as she gazed at the cabin.

"No, but it's closer to town than my place," Adrian said with a shrug. "I'll come stay overnight quite often."

Shawn laughed. "Yeah. We normally end up living together in one place or another quite often. Just depends on what mood we're in. But we keep both cabins because sometimes we just need our own space."

Jamie nodded. Her arms tightened around her duffel bag. "And the two of you are…?"

Adrian smirked, understanding what she was asking. Lots of people in town assumed that they were gay. But then, most people in Deville didn't care about what wolf culture was like, or that it was perfectly natural for wolves like them to have strong bonds of the same sex that were neither romantic nor sexual. Not exactly platonic in the strictest sense of the word, either.

"Bonded partners," Adrian nodded at Jamie. "In search of a shared mate."

"Right," Jamie whispered. Slowly she stepped toward the cabin and then stopped again.

She angled herself so she could see both him and Shawn as he rounded the truck. The duffel bag clutched in her arms looked almost like a shield as she peered from one to the other, fear clearly written in her eyes. Adrian wasn't entirely certain how he felt about that look. He didn't really like it, but he also didn't entirely dislike it, either.

Jamie swallowed hard and whispered, "And I'm here because…?"

Shawn leaned against the truck. "I think you can figure that one out."

A shudder rolled down Jamie's spine. Adrian stepped up beside her as his wolf growled low in pleasure. It always did like to see people shivering in anticipation, fearing the pleasure that was about to come upon them but fearing the denial even more. He had a feeling that in this situation, his wolf was misreading her cues for its own desire, though.

All her curves beckoned to him as he put a hand on her shoulder, gently guiding her away from the truck. She stumbled with him, her expression turning rather blank. He sighed. Absolute terror was not exactly the way to start this.

"You are promised to us," Adrian said. "That means that from now on, you belong to us. But we're not going to start demanding things right off the bat, Jamie. This *is* also because we wanted to get you away from that brute of a stepfather you have. Chloe is often ranting about it," he added so she didn't think they were soft. "And this is one way we can get her on our side a bit more. That way we can call in her favor whenever Sly is pissed with us."

He laughed here and so did Shawn, but Jamie's shoulders only tensed further.

"You're our promised mate," Shawn said slowly. "I can understand if you were hoping for a fated mate, but until such time that you find that mate, you're ours. But we'll take you on dates and whatnot when we have time. You're a wolf, you should be with the rest of the wolves, anyway."

Jamie flinched at that, making Adrian raise a brow. She certainly didn't seem to be very happy to be with her own kind. Adrian had to wonder what sort of bullshit she'd been fed in her life… he and the rest of the wolf shifters of Devil Mountain had been living here for almost ten years now and none of them had even known that Jamie was a shifter until a few months back when she had been caught up in a battle with a dragon shifter.

His hand slid down her back, and he felt her tense even more under his touch. "What are you so afraid of, Jamie?"

Her expression blanked out entirely into a numb sort of hollowness. She looked up at him, her arms falling loose at her sides. Shawn caught the duffel bag before it hit the ground and hoisted it up over his shoulder.

"I belong to you," Jamie said, her voice as hollow as her expression. "So what does that mean? What was promised to you? Promised mates. That means that you expect…"

She trailed off, shuddering. Adrian nodded, having realized that was what she was afraid of indeed. He'd done enough skulking around and finding out about her life to know she had a certain reputation. A reputation, he'd decided, that was undeserved. More like she was a magnet for sexual harassment. And while she was sexy and gorgeous and her curves had made their way into more than one dream, why so much of the town had conspired against her in particular was… unnerving.

They might not know she was a wolf, but as it turned out, everybody knew her father had been. Adrian could only guess that it was that prejudice rearing its ugly head toward Jamie, whether the town was aware of it or not.

"Of course, we expect sexual intimacy," he said bluntly because there was no use pussyfooting around the truth. "But like Shawn said, when we have time, we're going to take you on dates and approach this the right way. When we sleep together, it is going to be because you want us."

She flinched at that but said nothing more as they led her past the cabin and toward the hobbit hole in the back. It was fashioned after the set of Bag End in the Lord of the Rings movies. Gently curved roof with grass growing over it, a lovely round, green door in the front.

Inside was quite a bit smaller than the movie portrayed, though. It was tall enough for them, but was only a one-room place. A small kitchenette was tucked into the front left corner while a bathroom was in the back left corner. A desk under the full-sized window held room for a computer and printer and the bed against the back wall was only a twin-sized mattress. Drawers were built in underneath the bed.

Overall, big enough for one person so long as they didn't

have many possessions. With the three of them inside, though, it was crowded.

"This is where I'll be living?" Jamie asked doubtfully as Shawn tossed her duffel bag onto the bed. "Why here? Why not in the cabin?"

Shawn shrugged. "Because this is where we decided to put you. You're ours now, so we will take care of you. No rent, no bills, nothing. You're free to decorate this place as you wish and to use the kitchen and laundry in my cabin whenever you want. The woods are yours to explore, and if you want to garden or whatnot, all you have to do is tell me your plans."

Jamie nodded slowly, her brow furrowing. "I'll need my car. I didn't think of it. But I'll need it."

Adrian shook his head. "That old junker? Nope, we're selling it, and we'll get you a new car when we go into the city next. In the meantime, you want to go anywhere, Shawn or I will drive you."

"But... work..."

"You don't have to worry about working at the diner anymore." Adrian grinned, rather proud of himself. "We already told Bill that you won't be working for him anymore."

Jamie's cheeks flushed and her eyes flashed. It was the first real emotion she'd shown and so Adrian grinned wider, even if he was confused as to why she would be angry at not having to work for that bastard anymore. Bill was notorious for overworking and verbally abusing his staff. Many of his packmates' mates used to work for Bill, or still did, and they complained terribly about him. Of course, the occasional visit from the wolves toned down his attitude quite a bit, but Adrian didn't understand why they didn't just buy him out and run the place themselves.

Jamie twisted her hands in front of herself as she lifted her chin, trembling violently. "I don't care what my stepfather promised you. I am not going to sleep with you! I'm a virgin and I am going to stay a virgin until I am fully satisfied that I have found the right man to share my first time with. So. I'm not going to be your... your... *kept woman*."

Adrian considered her while Shawn smirked. His mood darkened as he watched her, considering the other reputation she had. A great deal of the town seemed to think that she had a sexual relationship with her stepfather and that was why she hadn't moved out all this time. Adrian didn't believe it, but if there was any truth... well, he could only assume that it wasn't willing on Jamie's part.

He shook those thoughts from his head. Now wasn't the time to contemplate what may or may not be happening in Jamie's life. She was here and promised to them, now. So, she was free of the boor of a stepfather she had anyway.

"You're a virgin, and you won't sleep with anybody you don't want to sleep with," Shawn agreed. "Which is why when you lose your virginity to us, it will be because you give it to us."

Adrian nodded his agreement, stepping up close behind her. His wolf whined, aching to get even closer. The conversation was pulling up some rather delightful images in his mind. He didn't touch her, not yet, just letting his presence soak into her.

"Now." Shawn slowly cupped his hand around Jamie's cheek. "I am going to kiss you and then Adrian is going to kiss you. Alright?"

Adrian's wolf growled, not liking being the second. Jamie was rigid. He could almost hear her heart thumping against her ribs. She gave the tiniest of nods and Shawn bent over her. She was so tiny compared to his partner! Adrian smiled, loving the sight of it. Her curves, her frame. So much shorter than either of them. Shawn brushed his lips over Jamie's softly and gently and so fast it wasn't much of a kiss at all.

Jamie was still blinking as though stunned when Adrian turned her and gave her the same sort of kiss. A promise that she would not be molested at the same time as a promise that she would, sooner or later, be begging them to fuck her. And it would be fucking. No gentle 'lovemaking' for them. It was going to be animal. Adrian felt a little bad thinking about what they were going to put her poor virgin body through, but he knew that when they were finished with her, she would be begging for more.

He stepped back, licking the taste of her off his lips, and smiled. Jamie stared up at him, that stunned expression still there.

"Is that... it?" she asked, wringing her hands.

"Did you want more?" Shawn asked.

She shook her head quickly, but there was still something in her eyes that told Adrian it wasn't entirely true.

"Now. We'll leave you to settle in," Shawn started, but Adrian stopped him.

"Wait. I think we might have given Jamie the wrong impression here. Tiny kisses and assurances that we won't touch her until she wants us to. The thing is," Adrian said, lacing his voice with authority, "we are going to be the ones who take your virginity, Jamie. We're going to pop your cherry and have you in ways that you can't possibly imagine, no matter how much porn you've watched."

Jamie's cheek flushed dark red. "I don't watch porn," she blurted.

"No?" Adrian rose a brow. "You'd better start. It'll give you some ideas about what you want to try out. Just remember that it does set unrealistic standards." He laughed at her embarrassment and headed for the door, Shawn close behind him. "Oh," he added once he was outside, "and we also have a bet as to who is going to seduce you first. So remember that."

He winked at her and walked away, grinning to himself. Beside him, Shawn punched his arm. "Way to freak her out."

"She needs to know what she's gotten into. It's not like we can go sexless forever."

Shawn rolled his eyes. "Whatever. I don't like the way you

were acting is all. Now let's go. Another hiker disappeared, and Sly wants us in the search grid."

Adrian cast one more look over his shoulder at the hobbit hole and sighed heavily. "Fine. Duty before pleasure I suppose."

CHAPTER THREE

Even though he knew it would be a rather large shock for Jamie to suddenly find herself with two promised mates, Shawn couldn't help but be a bit miffed at the way she stayed locked away in the hobbit hole. They had been clear enough in telling her what to expect, hadn't they? But she was hiding like a rabbit in her den. That wasn't the proper behavior of a wolf. Not even omegas were that cowed.

He knocked on the door, resisting his own wolf's urge to just stride in. It was his property, his promised mate. Everything here was his, why should he put boundaries in place? His scowl deepened as he heard no movement from the other side of the door. Jamie needed to stop hiding away like this. How was she ever meant to have a proper place in the pack if she refused to allow herself the freedom to explore?

"Jamie, open up," he ordered, knocking again.

The door creaked open ever so slightly and her terrified brown eyes peered up at him. Shawn frowned, not liking her to be so afraid. If there was fear he wanted it mingled with desire and then not the type of fear that meant she thought he was going to hurt her—at least, hurt her without her consent. He planned quite a rough introduction to the world of sex for her.

"Here." He passed her a bag of clothing that he'd bought in town that day. The clothes that she had were old and ratty. "Get showered and dressed. We're going to a barbeque up at Sly's place."

Jamie peered into the bag, worrying at her lower lip with her teeth. It was a seriously sexy sight. Shawn watched the way her teeth worked, and his skin tingled with the desire to have those teeth breaking his skin. He had to look away before it started to bulge his jeans.

"These aren't exactly my style," Jamie said as she lifted a tank top from the bag. "I don't usually go for… lace."

"Well, I'm not taking you anywhere when you're dressed like you picked through a charity's rejects. Get dressed." Shawn turned but stopped when Jamie called after him.

"Why are you taking me to a barbeque?" Her brows were drawn together, her cupid's bow lips pursed now. She searched his face as though looking for a hidden trick.

Shawn frowned back at her. "It's not a secret that you're living here, Jamie. Why wouldn't I take you to a barbeque? I told you that you should be with other wolves and that's how you're going to be with the other wolves. Besides that, Chloe has been on Adrian and me about asking you out for months now. Ever since you helped take care of me when I was injured."

He hated thinking about that time. The dragon that had attacked the pack put him on blockers, then beat him up so badly that he hadn't even been able to walk. That sort of helplessness still made him pull his lips back in a snarl. His wolf paced angrily. It wished they had been the ones to have killed that dragon, but unfortunately they hadn't had the chance. At least the wolves that had been enslaved by the dragon were now free and had joined the pack.

And really, he did owe Jamie for taking care of him. He had been in worse shape than he had let Adrian know and probably needed more care than he allowed himself to get.

He might have ended up being laid up for even longer than he was if Jamie hadn't been there, insisting on looking after him.

How could she have done that so willingly and without any thought to herself and then turn around and be terrified of him now? His wolf yipped at him, wanting him to go forward and claim her right now so she would know that she was never going to go back to her bastard stepfather. Shawn resisted. She belonged to him and Adrian, yes, but sometimes these things took time.

He sighed and tried to make his tone more persuasive, rather than commanding. "You have been holed up for days now. You took good care of me while I was injured. This is a way for me to pay you back. Everybody knows that you were miserable with your stepfather and now you don't have to deal with him. Unless you want us to kill him?"

Jamie's eyes widened. "No!"

"Well, then. Get showered and dressed and let's get a move on with this. Okay?"

But Jamie didn't move. "I only helped you when you were hurt because you were protecting me. You wouldn't have gotten hurt if you hadn't… you know, helped me."

"Then show your thanks by coming to this barbeque." He rolled his eyes, growing impatient. "I don't understand why you are being so reluctant about this."

Jamie licked her lips and his wolf zeroed in on her pink tongue. Were other parts of her body that same pink color? He wanted to know. *Patience,* he told his wolf as if growled. Adrian telling her they'd made a bet about her would put her on edge enough. As though she didn't know that they'd both be there when she lost her virginity.

"But why do you want me to come?" Jamie insisted as she put the tank top back into the clothing bag. "I don't get it. What am I supposed to do there?"

"Your entire book club will be there," Shawn replied, rapidly losing patience with this conversation. What was she supposed to do there? The same thing as all the rest of them. Eat, drink, chat. Hell, she could bring a book and sit over in the corner ignoring them all if she wanted to. It wasn't as though she had never been to one of these things before. Even when they didn't know she was a wolf, Chloe had brought her to some of their barbeques. "Do whatever you normally do at these things."

Jamie frowned at him. "But what am I supposed to tell them?"

"The truth."

"That my stepfather threw me away because his girlfriend doesn't like me? That you showed up and said that I belong to you and brought me up here without any notice, without even asking if I wanted anything to do with you?"

Shawn rolled his eyes. When she said it like that, it sounded like they'd kidnapped her, rather than making the arrangement. The rest of the wolves would understand. But, he mused, out of all her book club friends, only Sandra was likewise a wolf. The other women would not be pleased with Jamie talking about the arrangement like that. And then they'd whine to their mates, who in turn would be grumpy with Shawn and Adrian.

"Just tell them that your stepfather kicked you out and Adrian and I took you in. That you're living in the hobbit hole for the time being. Okay?" He turned back to her, increasing his frown. He added sarcastically, "Or is that going to be too complicated for you?"

Jamie dropped her gaze and shook her head. Her shoulders hunched inward. "No. They won't question why I was kicked out. It's not like I haven't tried to leave before."

"Exactly," Shawn grunted. "So I don't understand why you're acting like I'm dragging you to a guillotine. Adrian and I rescued you if nothing else, and we want to take you to a fucking barbeque where your friends are going to be. Stop making such a fuss over it."

He grunted again and turned back toward his cabin to get

ready but stopped again when she called once more. He turned, lips pursed in irritation. Jamie clutched the bag of new clothes to her chest. For a moment she was silent, as though she wasn't certain she actually wanted to speak. But just when he started to turn away once more, she blurted, "What does it mean to be promised mates?"

Shawn frowned. "We already told you that. You belong to us and we will be your mates unless such time arrives that you meet your fated mate."

"What is a fated mate?"

Shawn stared. How could she possibly not know what fated mates were! He scratched his head and scoffed. "Soulmates, basically. You know, the look into my eyes, I can't live without you crap."

"I don't believe in soulmates."

Shawn shrugged. "Whatever. But you're our promised mate, so you don't have to worry about it."

"But..." Jamie pulled in a deep breath. "But I am allowed to say no... right? I mean... I don't have to... say yes..."

Shawn frowned deeply at her. Hadn't she been listening to them when they told her that she'd want them before they fucked her? "You won't want to say no."

Jamie flinched. "Why are you so certain? I've heard it before. People who say that I want something when I don't want it and they try to force the matter. How are you so certain that I will want you, Shawn? Because I was nice to you? Because you're so certain that you're all that and a bag of chips?"

Shawn had to smile at that. It was ridiculous, really. 'All that and a bag of chips'. But of course, she was going to want them. She was a woman, they were men. They weren't related. She said she was saving herself for the 'right' man, but there was no such thing as the 'right' man. There was only the 'best' man. And they'd be patient with her, no matter how much his wolf was gnawing at his ribs and wanting him to go show her how good he actually would be for her.

"Are you a lesbian or asexual?" he asked calmly.

Jamie's cheeks reddened as she shook her head. "Sometimes I wish I was."

That made him frown. He hesitated a moment before slowly returning to her. "You wish you didn't find men attractive?"

"The guys in high school..." She trailed off and shuddered. "There are nice enough men out there, but none of the good ones would think twice about me except with pity."

"Pity?" Shawn laughed out loud. "You think that Adrian and I pity you?"

Jamie's cheeks went even redder and she ducked her head, looking absolutely miserable. "You said that you were doing this because I helped take care of you when you were injured. And I know I'm nothing to look at, I have heard that often enough. When men are interested, they're not interested in *me*. They just want a quick..." She trailed off and blinked rapidly.

Shawn stared in surprise. Her eyelashes were wet. What the fuck was this nonsense. He opened his mouth, wanting to say something, but closed it again when he realized he didn't know what to say.

"I guess people assuming that I'm fucking two of the sexiest guys in Deville is better than people assuming I'm fucking my stepfather." She wiped her face with a trembling hand, laughing bitterly.

Shawn caught her hand, holding it tightly as she looked up at him with surprised eyes. "People can assume all they want," he said, his voice deep and growling.

He was aware that his wolf was likewise growling. Wanting to hunt down all those boys from high school that had made her feel this way. And how much of it was from her stepfather? How many people who assumed that something was happening with him took two additional seconds to also remember that he'd known her as a child—and that any sort of sexual contact between Jamie and her stepfather would be him abusing her?

"When I say that you will want Adrian and me, I don't mean that we'll back you into a corner," he snarled. Jamie flinched even though his anger wasn't directed at her. "What I mean is that you are going to come to us. Understand?"

For a moment, he thought she was going to argue with him. Say that she was never going to come to them, that she didn't want any of this. But instead, she lowered her head and nodded meekly.

He released her hand and stepped back. Maybe she didn't understand but she would. "Okay. Now get dressed already. We're going to be late."

CHAPTER FOUR

Jamie released a pent-up breath, grateful to have a plate of food in her hands. Nobody had acted like it was weird that she had gotten out of the truck with Adrian and Shawn. The other women actually smiled and gave her a little bit of light teasing over it, in fact. Chloe had seemed especially pleased. Maybe her new 'promised mates' had told the truth when they said that she had been pushing them to pursue a relationship with Jamie.

Of course, the question did come up as to how all this came together. Jamie dutifully relayed the lie, that Adrian and Shawn had taken her in when her stepfather kicked her out. As though the two weren't linked together.

The other women were outraged and spent several minutes cursing out her stepfather. That actually did make Jamie feel a little better. Being able to say out loud that her stepfather was a bastard and verbalize at least some of her fears with this arrangement was better than nothing. She drank the beer that was offered her—perhaps a little more than she ought to—and kicked the ground.

"If he sells the farm, I'm going to sue him," she said and the others all nodded, even though they knew she would never do such a thing. It was nice to dream about, though.

"I don't blame you," Wanda put in. She shook her head, scowling fiercely as she adjusted the toddler in her arms. "He's such a fucking bastard!"

Angela gave her a piercing look. "Hey, language! Don't say that sort of thing around the twins; they're picking it up. Not to mention…" She nodded to where Tanya played with Miriam's nephews. Apparently, she had been getting into trouble at school for her foul language. Growing up isolated from the world, a slave to a dragon with only five hard-boiled adults for company had apparently taken its toll on her vocabulary.

Here, Lucy, Tanya's aunt, chuckled. "Oh, that's not the worst thing she has heard or said. I don't get why people make such a fuss over that. I mean, you have kids bullying each other, and instead of dealing with that, teachers crackdown on language that adults use all the time. Maybe I should teach her some Japanese curses."

"Okay but…" Angela shrugged. "It's just society, I guess."

"Anyway," Chloe put in as she set her own toddler down to go toddle to his fathers, "I'm just glad that Adrian and Shawn managed to convince you to come, Jamie. Getting out of the house and spending time with other people is exactly what you need."

"And it's not romantic, you say?" Miriam pressed. "You're just living there until you can find a new place?"

Jamie nodded. She hoped nobody noticed that she flinched as well. Finding a new place wasn't going to happen. What were they going to say when this continued to drag on and on and on? She drank some more beer as she internally sighed. Of course, she needed to explain to them why she hadn't been at the diner and why she wasn't going to go back. Really, why had Shawn and Adrian decided to take away her job? What was she supposed to do in the meantime? Did they just want her to be financially reliant on them?

"And are you hoping for anything romantic to happen?" Sandra said with a sly smile.

Jamie shook her head hard. This was one thing that at least she could start a bulwark against. She would make it clear to all her friends that she didn't want anything to happen with Shawn and Adrian. Then, if something did happen—she dreaded thinking that it might; she didn't know these men! And they clearly expected her to grant them access to her body—she would at least have them backing her up when she went to the police.

Although... she eyed the sheriff, Ian, who was now talking and laughing with Adrian. He was a member of the pack and wouldn't so easily turn against his own packmates. *But if his mate and sister were backing me up...*

She shook her head again, trying to dislodge those fears. She just had to trust that Shawn and Adrian meant what they said, that they wouldn't touch her until she wanted them to. *Although they certainly pressed kissing me straight away.*

But it hadn't been... bad. They had been rather quick and light, over almost before it started. And maybe she could have said no to them and had that been the end of it. Neither of the wolves had made any advances since then. Which was all well and good. Because that bit of her wolf that had woken up by the time they kissed her had liked it. And she thought it might like to try it again.

She did have blockers, which she had used before coming to the barbeque, but her supply was rather low. It was difficult dealing with her wolf. It was always shivering, growling, snapping. The first night, it kept waking her up as it pawed against her chest, making it difficult to breathe. She hated it. And wished that it would just go away forever.

"I suppose it's for the best," Chloe was sighing. "Especially since the women they'd signed up for with the Paranormal Marriage Agency arrived in town."

Jamie stared blankly at her. "What?"

"Beth and Jessica," Chloe continued, nodding. "Apparently they signed up just before all that trouble with the dragon went down." A dark look briefly washed over

Chloe's face, but it was gone in a moment and she returned to smiling brightly. "It took the agency quite a while to find women who were willing to move all the way out here, though. But now that they are here, Shawn and Adrian can finally get themselves some proper mates. I hope it lasts."

Jamie's mind reeled. They had said that this arrangement was partly to get Chloe off their backs about finding mates. But why did they need that when they had women being ordered in? *Like picking from a catalog. Of course. Why doesn't it surprise me?*

"But I thought they wanted to share a mate," Jamie blurted, while her mind whispered that maybe they were lying, and they wanted a different sort of threesome altogether.

"Well, maybe they were just doubling their chances of finding someone who will work out." Chloe shrugged. "But I'm surprised that you haven't seen them. I thought they were going to go out to Shawn's place today."

"Probably got lost," Sandra laughed. "They live on the worst road in Deville."

Jamie smiled and laughed and excused herself. Her stomach was feeling rather crampy all of a sudden and she didn't like it. She quickly escaped to the bathroom, where she locked the door and sat on the toilet with her head in her hands. She started shaking in a way that made her feel like she was about to fall apart. What was going on here? What did Shawn and Adrian really want from her?

Easy, that dark voice whispered at the back of her mind. *They want to use you up. Take your virginity and fuck you dry and then toss you aside for a new conquest. Didn't you hear how Shawn described promised mates? As soon as someone more interesting comes along you'll be out on your fat ass with nothing, not even your virtue.*

Her throat swelled painfully. If she told the other women what really happened, would they back her up? All of them seemed to be so happy with their mates. But what if it wasn't as rosy as she thought? She had heard lots of things about shifters growing up. How they were all sex obsessed. How the men liked to pass their women around like trading cards. How 'no' wasn't a word they understood or respected.

What if they all started out this way? She had thought some of the things that happened around here were strange. And then she and Wanda were kidnapped by that dragon. He had been planning such terrible things for them… and he'd said it, too. That when he took them, they'd want him to. Yes, it felt… different when Shawn and Adrian said it, but the words were the same. How could she trust them to actually listen to her when she said no?

And the other women had been hinting for some time that they thought she would be a good match for Shawn and Adrian. If she did tell them that they had come in and made a deal with her stepfather and that she now belonged to them…

They'd probably say it was a good thing because it meant they cared enough to take her away from her stepfather.

Bile rose in Jamie's throat. The truth of it was… they had done her a favor by taking her away from him. Even if the whole situation was terrifying to her, at least she didn't have to deal with her stepfather. Miranda might dislike that Jamie was an adult living with her stepfather, and there were rumors that she slept with him… and they weren't entirely untrue.

It only happened when he was really drunk. Normally she could see it coming and take off for a few hours until he was passed out, and she didn't have to deal with him. But sometimes he was already drunk when she came home. Then he would try to get her to drink with him. Try to get her to 'help him to bed'. It had never gone any further than him getting a little handsy and promising she'd enjoy it but all the same.

She told nobody. Even when her friends asked her point-blank if everything was okay. She just couldn't tell them.

She knew the way they'd look at her if she did. With pity and disgust. Jamie couldn't take that.

And now she was free of him… or at least as free as she could be for the moment. But was it really worth it when she didn't know what Shawn and Adrian's triggers were? She didn't know how to placate them. Didn't know their warning signs. So how did she protect herself against them?

There was a knock on the door. "Jamie? Are you okay?"

It was Lucy. Jamie sucked in a deep breath. She knew what had happened with Lucy when she was a slave to the dragon. If any of them would understand… Lucy would.

Slowly, Jamie pulled herself from the toilet. She opened the door, finding Lucy standing on the other side, looking tense and worried.

And Jamie couldn't say it. Because what if she was misreading the situation? What if Adrian and Shawn really were looking to help her out? Lucy had been through so much. She didn't deserve to have this slice of happiness she had found in Deville taken away from her. So Jamie smiled, pulling on the careful mask she had perfected through so many years of lies.

"I'm fine," she said. "Just feeling a bit sick to my stomach. I'm drinking too much." She stepped from the bathroom and made herself laugh. "I guess I'm still worked up about my stepfather. Let's go back to the barbeque."

Lucy nodded, though her brow was still furrowed. Jamie was grateful she didn't say anything else, giving her time to think. It wasn't long after that, though, that Jamie sought out Shawn and asked him to take her home. She was already exhausted, and she was drinking too much. She leaned her head against the cool glass of the window as Shawn pulled away.

"You okay?" he asked and there was a note of what sounded like genuine concern in his voice.

Jamie didn't reply—she still didn't know how he'd react if she told him no. So she wasn't going to tell him anything at all.

CHAPTER FIVE

Two more people disappeared from Deville over the next week. This time it wasn't just some out-of-town hikers, either. Both of these people were from Deville. They knew the area. Sly was getting more concerned. The disappearances had all the hallmarks of vampires, but there was no evidence of vampires being around. At first, when it seemed like there were just more stupid people around than usual, the wolves did more search and rescue stuff or patrolled the trails to make sure people weren't being idiots.

Now, Sly bumped things up to start really trying to figure out what was happening around here. That meant nightly patrols, which sometimes spilled over into the daylight hours. Sometimes, they even went to noon.

Adrian grumbled to himself as he emerged from the trees around Shawn's place. After spending so much time running up and down the mountain, he needed to relax. Shawn would be around shortly; he had diverted to show William and Jacob to the fork in the trails that would lead them down to town. They had a lot to talk about.

This whole thing with the disappearing hikers was getting worrisome. The town was getting nervous, and when they got nervous, tongues started wagging. If they didn't figure out what was happening here and put an end to it, then the next thing to happen would be fingers would start pointing at the wolf shifters of Devil Mountain. From there, it wouldn't take long for hostilities to bloom and for things to get really bad. So the best option right now was to figure out what the fuck was happening here.

If it was vampires, things would be easy to settle. But if it was vampires, that meant they weren't using the tunnels beneath the mountain and they were snatching people without any signs of struggles. Not leaving any scents behind, either.

Adrian growled as he retook his human form next to the cabin. After that long run, he wanted to have a nice soak in the hot tub. He pulled the cover off and then jogged to the hose hanging up on the side of the house, turning it on to spray the sweat and grime from his body. The water in the hose was nice and warm from the sunshine. He moaned as his tight muscles started to relax.

A small yelp caught his attention and he turned to see Jamie standing beside the hobbit hole. She had strung some line between the house and nearby tree. Several items of clothing hung from it already. A shirt dripped from her hands as she stared at him, wide-eyed. Her gaze was zeroed in on his groin, her lips in a small 'o'.

"Hello," he called, grinning when her head shot up.

Her gaze flickered to his face but returned to his groin. Her cheeks flushed a vivid red, and Adrian's stomach clenched as he imagined pushing himself into those pretty red lips. Her eyes went even bigger as his cock twitched with his arousal.

"Why so red in the face?" he called as he turned back, continuing to hose himself off. Only the hot water was gone, leaving him with cold water. He scowled at that. "You're a wolf shifter; don't you know we can't take our clothes with us when we shift from one form to the next?"

There was no answer. When he turned again, Jamie was

still standing there. Still holding the dripping shirt. Her eyes wide and her face red. She was no longer looking at him, though, but rather at the ground.

She might be a virgin, but she had to have seen a naked man before. She was a shifter, she couldn't have gone her whole life without interreacting with other shifters, as shifters!

He could see that he wasn't going to get any words from her while he was standing there naked, though, so he grunted with annoyance and turned off the hose. Stalking into the house, he grabbed a couple pairs of boxers from Shawn's dresser and pulled one set on before going back outside. Jamie was still there, although she had hung up the shirt by this time.

Adrian jumped into the hot tub and relaxed back, sighing in contentment. "You should come in, too," he called to Jamie. "Day like this. A good soak is worth it."

Jamie squeaked. It might have been a protest or her saying no. She mumbled something he couldn't understand and then turned. She bolted toward the hobbit house... Only Shawn had emerged from the trees behind her and she ran smack into him. She let out a blood-curdling scream as she jerked backward, nearly tripping.

"Whoa!" Shawn caught her arm and pulled her upright. "Why are you in such a hurry."

Jamie slapped both her hands over her mouth as she leapt back from him again. Her eyes were on Shawn's cock this time. Adrian shook his head. Maybe they had underestimated just how virginal Jamie actually was! She claimed not to have watched porn and seeing her reaction to a couple of naked men here... he believed it.

"There are some shorts over here," he called to Shawn. "Jamie is a little embarrassed by nakedness, it seems."

"Really?" Shawn's brow creased as he headed to the hot tub. "Have you never seen a naked man before? You're a wolf shifter!"

"But she has hidden her shifter abilities for most of her

life," Adrian pointed out as the thought dawned on him. "Just put them on so she's not standing there looking like we have a couple of snakes that are going to bite her."

Shawn grumbled under his breath. "My snake would like to bite her." He hosed himself off as Jamie slowly returned to her laundry.

Adrian grunted and leaned on the side of the hot tub. "Jamie. That can wait. Come join us for a soak."

"But I don't have a bathing suit," she blurted. Still not looking at them.

Shawn pulled on his boxers and marched over to her. He grabbed her arm and tugged her toward the hot tub. "You don't need a bathing suit. Just wear your underwear. We are."

She was breathing heavily, her breasts rising and falling, when Shawn released her. He climbed into the hot tub himself, shaking his head at her. Jamie grasped the hem of her shirt, her thighs pressed together tightly. As though she thought they were going to suddenly yank her legs apart. But... Adrian sniffed the air. That wasn't just fear she was feeling. He could smell the sweet, musky scent of arousal on her. It wasn't all him and Shawn, that was for certain.

"Well?" Shawn asked as he settled himself down. "Are you joining us or not?"

"I..." Jamie twisted the hem of her shirt between her hands, shifting from side to side. "I don't understand."

"You don't understand what?" Shawn frowned at her. "You don't understand hot tubs?"

"No, I meant... you signed up for that Paranormal Marriage Agency. Beth and Jessica are here in Deville because you... ordered them online. Like buying a new toy from a catalog."

Adrian shook his head. "There was a mix-up. Shawn and I did sign up for the agency, but neither of us placed any orders. We didn't send for Beth and Jessica at all. We're looking at getting it all straightened out." He stretched his sore muscles and leaned back on the opposite side of the tub. "Actually, the only reason we signed up in the first place was because we were trying to get Chloe off our backs. She's a great girl and I like having her as our alpha's mate, but she can be a little… overly mothering at times. Although she's gotten better since she had the baby."

"He's so cute," Shawn laughed as he set the timer for the jets. "I can't wait until he starts talking so we can teach him all sorts of curses. Chloe is gonna hate us."

Adrian laughed in agreement.

"But Beth and Jessica," Jamie insisted. "What are you going to do about them?"

"What are we supposed to do about them?" Shawn frowned at her. His irritation was showing through. "The agency sent them here by accident. The agency is going to take care of them. Now, are you going to come in here or not?"

"I…" Jamie looked at him and then at Adrian. She didn't meet his eye, her gaze traveling down his body to the body part that was covered by cloth and water. Her eyes darkened, the smell of arousal growing thicker.

It wasn't the only thing that grew, either. Adrian hardened at the desire so clear on her face. He held his breath for fear of showing just how much he wanted her. Because it wasn't just arousal that he saw. She was afraid, too. Why, he didn't understand. Sex was a normal and rather exciting part of life. What had happened to her to damage her views on something so natural, make it seem dirty and gross?

He had a feeling that it was due to the man who claimed to have raised her. And his wolf growled, torn between wanting to put his hands on Jamie and making her forget all the fears she had and seeking out her stepfather to punch his face into his skull. If there was any proof of his suspicions, he would have done it already. But no point in getting the pack into trouble with the locals unless they had proof to back them up.

He opened his mouth, about to tell her if she didn't want to get in she didn't have to, but Shawn interrupted him before he could start.

"Get in," Shawn ordered.

Jamie shivered. She took a deep breath—and started pulling off her clothes.

CHAPTER SIX

Shawn greedily eyed Jamie's body as it was revealed to him. Her movements were jerky, her cheeks flushed and her eyes dark. She chewed on her lip and trembled like she was going to bolt at any moment, but she removed her shirt and skirt. She wore black underwear that were more modest than plenty of bikinis, as well as a star-patterned bra underneath a blue tank top.

Shawn and Adrian shared a smile, enjoying the sight of her. While normally she wore things so baggy that her curves were obscured, this combo showed off her figure beautifully. Jamie hurriedly jumped into the hot tub, hunkering down in the bubbles caused by the jets. Her chin dipped into the water and her brown hair fell about her face, hiding it from them.

Shawn nodded once in satisfaction. He'd have preferred to see her relaxed here, but that would come in time. The hot water swirled around him, easing the stiffness of his muscles. His shoulders relaxed, and he let his eyes drift half-shut though he continued to peer at Jamie through his lashes. She was so tightly wound that she was going to cause her muscles to seize up.

Opening his eyes again, he cleared his throat. "You don't

have to be all wrapped up in on yourself like that, you know," he said. "You're more covered than if you were wearing a bikini."

"I don't wear bikinis," Jamie replied automatically, a defensive note in her tone. As though it was somehow… shameful?

Shawn frowned at her for a moment but broke into a laugh and smile quickly enough. If she was ashamed of her body, that would account for it alright. She probably bought into fashion magazines telling her that she needed to drop weight to have a 'swimsuit body'. He winked at her. "Ah, I see. You're afraid that all the other women at the beach or pool would stop being your friends."

Jamie looked up at him, startled.

"Because you're so fucking sexy," he continued, leaning his head back. He closed his eyes again. "Curves on curves. That hourglass figure. With those sparkling eyes and full lips of yours, you'd be strutting down the beach like a runway model and all their men would be drooling over you. That would make the other women mad, wouldn't it? Because who'd want to go for them when you're right there?"

As he spoke, he imagined her lounging on a beach in a string bikini. Her breasts large and round against the fabric, her smooth creamy skin exposed to him. Then he imagined that there was nobody on that beach other than him, Jamie and Adrian. And her mouth was against Adrian's, her legs spread open for Shawn as he kissed up her thigh, making her shiver in delight. If there was a palm tree they'd tie her to it and take turns filling her with their pleasure, until all three were spent and exhausted. Then they'd clean themselves up in the tepid waters of the ocean.

"I don't like bikinis," Jamie murmured.

Shawn opened his eyes, desire sweeping through him when he saw her warm brown eyes peering at him. She wasn't so hunched, her shoulders back a little more, her arms falling to her sides. One look at Adrian showed Shawn that his partner's eyes were heavily focused on Jamie. His eyes dark with lust, his shoulders rigid as he held himself back from her.

Well, Shawn wasn't exactly the type of person to deny himself when he saw something he wanted. So he reached for Jamie. She stared at him uncomprehending but didn't resist as he pulled her into his lap. He caught her mouth in a deep kiss, the heat from the hot tub soaking through him. He hardened rapidly, his hands on her hips as he explored her mouth with his tongue. She responded awkwardly, fumbling. Uncertain.

Adrian groaned and pushed himself to her other side, kissing her neck and suckling at her skin. Shawn continued kissing her. Her hands pressed against his chest, leaning into him. Her breath came more rapidly. He parted her legs, bringing her to straddle him. With an upward thrust, he ground his erection between her thighs—

And she pulled away from them like they'd pulled a gun on her and burst into tears.

Shawn sat there, stunned, as she wrapped her arms around herself again. She was even more tightly wound, her muscles as hard as stone and not in a good way. Tears poured down her face as she closed her eyes.

"Please don't make me," she begged, her voice breaking. "Your bet doesn't mean this does it?"

Bet? What bet? Shawn wracked his brains—oh. The bet they'd told her about, who would sleep with her first. His hands were still on her hips but lightly now. He shared a puzzled glance with Adrian. What had brought this on? They had been enjoying themselves. *She* had been enjoying *herself!* She had kissed him back...

Adrian heaved a sigh, shaking his head. Shawn wasn't entirely certain who he was annoyed with at the moment, though. A scowl crossed his own face as Adrian lifted Jamie off of his lap and put her back on the opposite side of the hot tub. He returned to his own place and Shawn's hands clenched and released, frustration welling in him. So Jamie got him hard and ready and then… what? Just chickened out?

"Why are you crying?" he snapped at her.

Perhaps not the best way to calm her down, but Shawn was never good at that sort of thing. He clenched his hands again. If Jamie didn't want any part of them the least she could do was have the decency to go ahead and say it! Not start kissing him back. Not look at them like that, not smell like she did and then start crying and saying that they were 'making' her. They weren't making her do anything!

Jamie hid her face in her hands and sobbed all the harder.

Adrian gave him an annoyed look as he turned off the jets. "Maybe it would be better if you left."

"I'm not going anywhere," Shawn spat back, incensed. "This is my home, my property. If you don't want to be around me, you can leave!"

"I wasn't talking to you, idiot," Adrian snapped back. "I was talking to the sobbing woman who would clearly rather not be around us."

"And why would she rather not be around us?" Shawn turned a glare back at Jamie.

She pressed her hands tighter to her face, still crying.

"I think I know why," Shawn continued, his hands clenching once more. He struggled to remain calm, but his wolf growled and snapped and paced restlessly. It wanted her. It wanted to see her laid bare before him, to taste her again, to feel just how good she was. And it also wanted to rip his face off for making her cry. He ground his teeth together as he pulled himself out of the tub.

"Calm down," Adrian rumbled.

Shawn glared at him. "Fuck you!"

"I wasn't talking to you," Adrian snapped at him. "But while we're at it, yeah. You can calm the fuck down, too!"

"I'll calm down when I'm ready to calm down. 'Cause the way I figure it, two things are going on here. Either Jamie here has put all her self-worth in the fact that she's a virgin and is freaking out because she wants to have sex, or she's trying to manipulate us into doing something for her. So what is it, Jamie?" He looked around for a towel only to remember that they hadn't brought any out. He leaned against the side of the hot tub and glowered at her, even though she couldn't see him. "Are you pulling a con or are you afraid of your own desires?"

Her head lifted. The tears were still streaming down her face as she stared at him incredulously. Then anger flickered in her eyes. Her hands dropped and she shot upright, standing with her fists clenched at her sides. "I'm afraid of *you*."

Shawn took a step back, surprised at her forcefulness. His wolf snarled, beating against his ribs. He tried to push the stupid thing aside. Now was not the time for it. "What the hell are you talking about? We told you that we weren't going to have sex until you wanted it!"

"And everything you've done has been acting like you're the one who gets to decide that, not me!" Jamie shrieked again. "You keep saying that I'm promised to you, that I belong to you! You talk about me stealing other women's men, like I'm some sex-obsessed nymphomaniac! You grab me and start kissing me without asking and then you try to say that you aren't going to do anything without me wanting it? But you never asked me if I wanted you to kiss me!"

Shawn spluttered, not having expected this verbal assault. "It's not the same! Besides, you enjoyed—"

"YOU DON'T GET TO TELL ME WHAT I ENJOYED!" Jamie's cheeks were flushed dark red, her fists trembling like she wanted to lash out.

Fresh, hot tears ran down her face. She jumped from the hot tub but snagged her foot. Shawn leapt forward to catch her, and she jerked away from him. If Adrian hadn't come from the other side, she would have tumbled face-first into the dirt. Even as he steadied her, though, Jamie yanked herself free of him. She rammed a fist into his shoulder and backed away from the both of them, panting like a rabbit cornered by a fox.

This was not how a wolf was meant to act. Shawn stepped back, giving her space. What the fucking hell had happened to her in her life?

"You don't get to decide whether I want something or not," Jamie gasped, her shoulders starting to curl inward again. "You don't get to decide what is too far. You don't get to decide any of that! None of you wolves get to decide that!"

Her hand moved to the center of her chest, pressing hard to her sternum. Shawn swallowed, holding up his hands. He had no idea what to say, though, and so remained silent.

Adrian, however, pulled himself from the hot tub and murmured, "Sorry. We didn't mean to scare you. To us, that was just kissing."

"It was not," Jamie replied, but the anger had left her voice. She wrapped her arms around herself like a shield. "I know it wasn't just kissing. I... *felt* it."

Shawn glanced down at himself. His erection was gone. No wonder with all the shouting. His brow furrowed. "But you were kissing me back."

"I didn't want you to get angry with me," Jamie murmured hollowly.

Was it true? He looked at Adrian, hoping that his partner would have a better idea of what was going on here. If it was all just because she was afraid of them... why had he smelled desire on her? So clearly, she was not willing to admit her own body's desires.

"It's not just that, though, is it?" He stepped forward and then rolled his eyes and stepped back when Adrian flashed a fang at him. "You did like it, didn't you? And you liked seeing us naked. I could smell that you were aroused. Whether or not you wanted to be," he added lifting his hands when Adrian snarled, "you were. But I guess that isn't good enough, huh? You gotta have that arousal and *want* to be aroused. You know what I think?"

She remained quiet.

Adrian gave him a warning look, but Shawn pressed on. "I think that you have trauma around sex. I think that you have preconceived notions of what it means to want sex and what having sex means. I think that you're a virgin because you've had to tightly protect yourself against people who would use sex as a weapon against you. And that you don't realize just how much they've destroyed your sexuality. So, what I think is that you need to go ahead and get some toys and take mastery of your own body, so it doesn't freak you out to be sexually aroused."

He turned on his heel and walked away before either Jamie or Adrian could reply. His wolf growled darkly but didn't press him to do anything in particular. He stalked into the house, grumbling under his breath as he did so. This arrangement was not going how he had wanted. Maybe it was a mistake to get mixed up with it all. They ought to have just stuck with the girls from the Paranormal Marriage Agency.

"Good work, genius," Adrian growled from behind him. "Jamie tells us not to tell her how she feels, and you turn around and tell her how she feels. Excellent work."

"I'm right," Shawn snarled back. He marched to the bathroom and grabbed a towel. "And you know I'm right."

"Fuck you," Adrian snapped, snatching the towel from him. "You've just set us back to the stone age. Good luck in your future endeavors."

Shawn snarled back, grabbing another towel. It wasn't his fault that Jamie had reacted that way. The thought came to him unbidden—maybe it wasn't Jamie's fault, either.

CHAPTER SEVEN

The sound of a baying wolf jolted Jamie upright. Her heart pounded in her chest as her gaze swept across the dark hobbit hole. From beyond the windows was utter blackness, the same darkness that was inside of the little house. The wolf's howls still rang in her ears, but now she recognized it wasn't a wolf outside but rather her own wolf in her chest. It batted at her ribs, biting and clawing. In a state of terror and fury at the same time.

Jamie gripped the blankets tightly as another sound came to her. The slow scrape of a chair being dragged across the floor. Soft footsteps. The breathing of another person.

Fear wrapped around her throat, a sense of utter dread filling her. A chill swept over her arms. She wasn't alone. There was someone in here with her! She froze, her eyes scraping the darkness, trying to see where they were. But it was only dark on dark on dark. Her blood rushed in her ears.

Another wash of cold made her hair stand on end, and she lunged for the switch above her bed. The lights burst on, flooding the room with brightness. Jamie swung out of bed, her hands lifted and ready to defend herself.

Only there wasn't anybody else in the hobbit hole at all.

Jamie blinked rapidly as she glanced around. Everything was exactly in order. The chairs weren't moved. The blinds were drawn. The door was locked. Even the bathroom was empty. There was nobody in this room with her.

Slowly, she lowered her hands, even though her heart was still pounding. She must have been having a nightmare. Licking her lips, she went to the door and checked it, just in case. It held firm and steady. She double-checked the bathroom, then looked in the cupboard and under the table. Nobody could actually hide in those places, but she still had the creepy feeling that there was someone else in here. There wasn't, she knew that.

But as she climbed back into her bed, she was hit by the desire to be with someone else. Not to be alone. Her wolf no longer darted all over the place, instead curling into a ball in the center of her chest and shivering like a rabbit. For once, she wished that it would be a little more assertive.

The memory of when she was a child came back to her. The way she and her wolf used to play together. The way they'd run through the fields, as one spirit. The way it urged her to climb trees and sing and dance and play without abandon. But that had all changed when she actually started shifting. She couldn't remember the exact words her stepfather had used to talk about her when he first caught her in her wolf form.

She did, however, remember the way he'd looked at her after that. And the way her mother told her it wasn't appropriate.

Now, her wolf was of no comfort to her at all.

Jamie glanced nervously over the hobbit hole again and shook her head. It might be silly, but she really didn't want to be here by herself. That creepy sense of not being alone was still there, and her wolf shivering like this didn't help matters. So she grabbed her phone and, before she could second-guess herself, called Shawn.

She knew that he might get the wrong idea. And she knew

that her wolf, perking up from where it shuddered in fear, might also get the wrong idea. But she didn't really care. She tried not to think of the feelings of heat and sparks under her skin when he'd kissed her. Tried not to think of how her wolf had pawed at her, trying to get her to go deeper. How she had longed to lose herself in his embrace while Adrian kissed on her from behind.

Or the epic meltdown she had had afterward.

Shawn answered on the second ring. "What do you want?" he snapped, not sounding sleepy at all.

Jamie flinched. Not that she blamed him for being upset, but it did make it rather difficult. The idea of being alone in this hobbit hole was even more frightening than facing him, however, so she murmured, "Can you come and bring me to your cabin?"

Shawn grumbled and hung up, but it was only a few minutes later that there was a knock on the door. Jamie, realizing that she hadn't bothered to dress, pulled a sweater over her pajamas and crept to the door, checking to make sure it was Shawn before she unlocked it. He gestured at her to follow him to the cabin.

"Is this a late-night booty call?" he asked, his tone teasing.

"No," Jamie muttered, ducking her head. "I… had a bad dream and didn't want to be alone."

Shawn gave her an incredulous look.

"I'm not used to being in a house by myself," Jamie defended herself. "And it was a really bad dream, okay? I dreamt that something was in there with me and it was breathing and moving chairs and I couldn't see it. It just really freaked me out."

"It must have." His face fell into a scowl. "Well, I suppose it's a good thing I'm not as terrifying as a nightmare."

Jamie flinched as they got to the cabin. He held the door open and she went through, blushing now as she remembered his… suggestion. *I wouldn't even know where to start with sex toys.* Her blush deepened, and she was glad that Shawn couldn't hear her thoughts. *I'm not even sure I know how to masturbate properly.*

Thinking about sexual things helped to ease the dread she still felt sticking to her skin, no matter how embarrassing it was. Even though she didn't necessarily want to think about it, she still wondered… what if Shawn was right? What if the reason she reacted to these things was because of sexual trauma? She hadn't been assaulted but…

But I have been. She chewed her lip as she entered the kitchen-living room area to find Adrian sitting at the table with a bunch of folders spread out before him. *Isn't it assault when people grab me and kiss me and I'm trying to stop them and they ignore me?*

That happened before. As Adrian lifted his head, turning a puzzled look on her, she folded in on herself again. Her wolf curled, nosing her toward him. It wanted her to wrap herself in his embrace. But she didn't want to—or if she did want to, she wasn't ready to. She didn't know. But as she gazed at him, she couldn't help but think about the hot tub again. The way their bodies had pressed to hers, the expert kisses that Shawn had given her.

I wouldn't call that assault. I did kiss him back. And they stopped when I pushed away. I did want them to kiss me like that. I just didn't want to… it went too far too fast. If Shawn had just been satisfied kissing, it would have been fine.

"Bad dream," Shawn said as he crossed behind her to pick up some of the folders. "So I guess we're not as bad as that."

Adrian gave him an annoyed glance then focused on Jamie again. "Do you want anything to eat or drink?"

Jamie shook her head, fidgeting awkwardly. Now that she was here, what was she supposed to do? "What are you both doing still awake?" she blurted.

"Just getting a little work done," Adrian replied.

"Yeah and then we have a couple of life-sized silicone dolls we like to play with," Shawn added, a petulant note to his voice.

"Silicone?" Jamie replied, her brow furrowing. What was

he—oh. Her eyes widened and heat flared in her cheeks. He was talking about sex dolls.

Adrian nodded as though this was the most natural conversation in the world. "It's easier to work with the silicone than finding real women that like the same things we like."

Jamie held up her hands as though to ward off the conversation. "I don't need to have that sort of information."

Shawn snorted, but Adrian frowned. He was the one who wasn't so pushy about it all, so it surprised Jamie when he said, "Maybe it is information that you need. Think about this situation we are in. Shawn and I expect to sleep with you eventually. But we're not in any great rush. Yes, real skin is better than silicone, but when it comes down to it, we are very capable of taking care of ourselves. You don't have to feel pressured, Jamie. We have to give you as much space as you want. Or, if you feel like you're not brave enough to make the first move, we can continue to build toward it. Just not as quickly as we did in the hot tub."

She sank down at the table and chewed on her thumb. It would be best if she could actually talk to them about this, right? "But you can't say that you expect me to sleep with you in one breath and in the next say I don't have to feel pressured. The expectation is pressure itself."

"She has a good point," Shawn said, smirking. He was so relaxed.

Jamie wished she knew how to read him better. Then, bolstering herself, "And you can't get mad at me for pushing you away and then say that I don't have to feel pressured."

Shawn's smile disappeared. "I wasn't mad because you pushed me away."

"You started yelling at me."

"I was mad because you said *don't make me*. As though we were about to rape you. If you didn't want us to kiss you, you should have just said no."

Jamie flushed. She opened her mouth and closed it again, not knowing how to explain what she was feeling. It was all so confusing! Eventually she ran her fingers through her hair and shook her head. "I didn't expect you to be... like how you were. I got scared. I'm not used to men being like that unless they want to try to... force the issue. I'm not just some flesh and blood doll to play with. I don't want to have sex just for the sake of having sex and I don't want men to look at me as though sex is all I'm good for!"

She hid her face in her arms at the end of her outburst. Why couldn't she just hold her tongue around these two? Now they were going to be angry with her again. How much of this could they take before they just threw her out on her ass like she deserved? Her shoulders shook as she fought to regain control of herself while her wolf growled—actually growled! What was it growling at her for?

A long, low growl came from one of the wolves. Jamie flinched. It seemed that she had gone too far already. But when a hand rested on her arm, it was gentle. And when she looked up, she found both of them working to control their anger.

Shawn was the first one to speak. "Who was it?"

She remained silent, not understanding.

"You said that men tried to *force the issue*. Who was it? You don't deserve that sort of treatment; we'll make sure nobody does that to you again." Fury burned in his eyes, but despite her initial reaction, Jamie knew it wasn't directed at her. Could it be possible that they were angry... *for* her? Instead of *at her*?

"I'm tired," she whispered because after the hot tub and then that disturbing dream and now with her wolf fully there and no blockers to suppress it, she couldn't deal with this, too. Her brain was just too heavy. "Can I sleep on the couch?"

"Yeah," Shawn muttered. "I'll get you a blanket."

CHAPTER EIGHT

Adrian considered Jamie as she slept on the couch while he quietly made coffee. After the blowup at the hot tub and then their continued conversation that night, he had been expecting her to demand that they take her to a hotel or something to sleep. Now, seeing her so deeply asleep on the couch, it made him frown. There was more to her life than they knew—although he had a pretty good guess as to what it was she was keeping a secret.

Her admission the previous night, that she had been assaulted in the past, made his blood boil. If she had named any names, he would have hunted those men down and made certain they paid. She didn't deserve that sort of treatment!

But it explains why she reacted to us the way she did, he thought, pouring himself a coffee and adding in the cream and sugar he liked. *We have to be more careful. We can't assume that if she doesn't want something she'll say no. And we can't just take physical cues, either. We're going to have to ask with every step.*

He scowled, but it was the only thing to do. Jamie was terrified of them. Sure, he knew that she was attracted to them, and he knew that if she let herself go, they'd have all slept in the same bed last night. But the fact of the matter was that Jamie clearly did not trust herself. And if she didn't trust herself, how could she trust them?

This was the most relaxed he had ever seen her. And even so, she was still rigid in sleep, still curled into herself, protecting herself.

And once more he wondered if there was truth to the rumors about her stepfather. She was a virgin, that was certain, but that didn't mean that her stepfather hadn't molested her in other ways.

Shawn came padding down the hallway, his phone in his hand. He took Adrian's coffee without asking. Adrian rolled his eyes but fixed himself a new cup and jerked his head to outside, so they wouldn't disturb Jamie. Shawn glanced at her, regret flashing across his face, and followed Adrian out.

"Jacob called," Shawn said once they were outside. "He wants us to run over to Lucy's cabin. Apparently some stuff happened over there that freaked her out, but Tanya is throwing a temper tantrum about school and they want to take care of her." He shrugged. "Clinton and Trevor are still on patrol and we're the closest."

Adrian sighed. "Guess we'd better tell Jamie that we're heading out, then."

Shawn frowned at him. "No. We're not going to tell her that. We're going to let her sleep."

Adrian frowned right back at him, but it was a reasonable statement, he supposed. Jamie did need sleep after all. It was just weird for Shawn of all people to be thinking of someone other than himself when they weren't in a life-threatening situation. He'd throw himself in front of a bullet without thinking, but he also stole coffee and refused to wash dishes.

Pointing that out, though, would only cause an argument and so Adrian shrugged. They drove over the mountain to Lucy's cabin, which was bigger than Adrian had expected. He'd never had reason to come here before, but it was two stories and looked large enough to house not only Lucy but also the other wolves they'd rescued from the dragon a few months back. It made sense, he mused, since they were all practically family. Tanya called her aunt after all. He wasn't certain just what the biological relationships of their new packmates were. Not that it mattered.

He frowned when he saw two unfamiliar women sitting on the porch with no sign of Lucy. The two of them jumped to their feet, looking eager. Then it clicked.

Beth Perkins and Jessica Byrd. Sly had told him about them at the barbeque. Women sent by the Paranormal Marriage Agency to be their mail-order brides.

"Fuck," Adrian muttered under his breath. How long had they been here now? And this was the first time he was meeting them. "Fuck, fuck, fuck!"

Shawn gave him a concerned look but didn't speak.

Adrian sighed internally as he headed for the porch. What had he been thinking about Shawn being unconcerned with others? *Pot, meet kettle*. He managed a smile as he trotted up to the porch and nodded at them.

"Ladies," he greeted. "We got a call saying something was amiss around here?"

"There was a prowler," one of the women blurted. "Lucy had to go to work and didn't have time to look around. You know, in her wolf form." She fidgeted, twisting her hands while her gaze was locked on Adrian's face. "I'm Jessica, by the way. We've been meaning to come see you but— "

"Why?" Shawn interrupted. His brow furrowed as he looked over them. "And why are you staying with Lucy?"

Adrian sighed heavily. "I told you about this. Jessica and Beth were sent by the Paranormal Marriage Agency. Although by now I thought you would have gotten your tickets to go back home," he continued, glancing back at the women who both looked stunned. "You see, there was a mix-up. Shawn and I did not apply for you to come here. In fact, I'm not sure we finished our applications to join the marriage agency. We've found someone else."

Jessica's shoulders slumped. She fell back into the chair on the porch while Beth pressed her hands to her cheeks as they grew pink.

"I'm sure the agency will take care of this," Adrian continued as Shawn shifted uncomfortably beside him. "It's good that you have found a place to stay in the meantime."

Neither of the women replied to that. Since there was nothing else to say, Shawn and Adrian went into the woods and shifted, checking for prints and scents and other things that would indicate human or animal around the area. It was unusually cold and there was a faint bitter scent to the air that Adrian couldn't quite catch. After several hours, he and Shawn reconvened at the house.

Beth and Jessica were still on the porch with their coffees, both looking unsettled and nervous. Jessica especially looked like she had been crying. Adrian flinched, but what was he supposed to do? The Agency never told him or Shawn that they were coming, and they hadn't ordered them anyway. There had been a serious screw-up somewhere—the women were probably entitled to compensation.

Adrian finished buttoning his shirt as he jumped up the stairs and leaned against the railing. "We didn't find anything. What sort of prowler did you see?"

"We didn't actually see anything," Beth murmured. "But we all woke up suddenly thinking there was someone in the house. Even Lucy, and she's a wolf," she added, as though Lucy being a wolf meant she was immune to fits of paranoia. "We turned on all the lights, but it was so dark outside, and we kept hearing things, like fingers tapping against the glass. It was really scary. And Lucy doesn't seem like the kind of person to scare easily."

"She doesn't," Shawn agreed. His face pulled into a frown as he turned to Adrian. "That's kind of like the nightmare Jamie said she had. Do you think it could be connected?"

Adrian shrugged. "I've never heard of contagious nightmares before. Besides, these ladies say something was there and Jamie only had a bad dream."

"Jamie?" Jessica said, a jealous note in her voice. "She's the one you decided on, is she? Did you get her through the agency?"

Adrian sighed. "No. Our arrangement with Jamie is not quite like that."

"Arrangement?" she leaned forward, her eyes lightening. "So it's not love?"

"It's not your business, either," Shawn interrupted. He frowned at Jessica and then at Beth. "Look, it sucks that you were dragged all the way out here for no reason, but that's just how it is. Adrian and I aren't interested. Though, God only knows why not." He kicked the ground and scowled. "For fuck's sake, look at you! If it weren't for Jamie, I'd be all over the both of you. At least I'd be asking if you like to get fucked rough. But I'm not even interested! *Fuck*."

Shawn spun on his heel and stalked away, disappearing into the trees again. Adrian looked to the sky, praying for strength. What about the situation had made any of that reasonable to say? Although… he had to admit that now that Shawn said it, he got where he was coming from. Beth and Jessica both had the curves of Hilda from the pin-up calendar. Normally, they'd be the kind of women that he'd be all smiles with, the kind of women that he'd try to entice to bed for the sort of fucking that he and Shawn enjoyed. Their soft skin and plump bodies were far more enticing than the silicone dolls they had, after all.

But in comparison to Jamie? He didn't even have the desire to see how ripe they were. And his wolf couldn't care less, batting at his ribs to get him to run back over the mountain and take Jamie in his arms. Surely if they were able to talk and reassure her some more, she'd understand that she was safe with them…

Adrian coughed and shook his head. "Sorry about that. My

partner doesn't always think before he speaks. But I'm certain that you will receive lots of luck as you continue to go forward with the Paranormal Marriage Agency. In the meantime, if you're looking for work, there is always the diner that Lucy works at. I wouldn't suggest it unless all of you were going to join forces and force Bill into treating you like human beings, though."

He smiled his most charming smile at them, but neither seemed swayed. Well, he couldn't exactly blame them for that, either. Beth looked on the verge of tears while Jessica's face was turned toward the forest like she wanted to run off into it and disappear forever.

"Look," he continued, trying to be gentle about this, "I am sorry that your expectations were not met here. Angela has a nice little farm if you wanted to work with someone less toxic than Bill, but I'm not sure she can pay much. Other than that, all I can suggest is that you contact the agency and explain the situation."

His cellphone started to ring, and he shrugged at the women, not sure what else to say, and headed for the truck where Shawn already was. They hadn't found anything, so there wasn't much point in staying any longer.

"Adrian?" Jamie's voice came through the phone, sounding frightened. "Where are you?"

"We had to go check on something for some friends," he replied, frowning. "Are you okay?"

A beat of silence answered and then, "Oh. I just wanted to know… okay, thanks."

She hung up without another word. Adrian frowned at his phone, then snorted and tossed it onto the back seat as he buckled up. "That was weird."

Shawn shoved the truck into gear. "Yeah, well it's not our fault. It's the agency's fault."

"No, I meant…" Adrian shook his head. "Never mind. It doesn't matter. Let's go to the diner. I want to hear from Lucy what happened last night. And maybe check out a few more of the trails before heading home."

Shawn grunted, the only agreement that Adrian got, and they headed out. But Adrian didn't like the chill that stole down his spine, nor the way his wolf snarled and snapped, like there was an enemy lurking nearby that he couldn't quite see.

CHAPTER NINE

The next few days were torturously slow. The only good thing to happen was that Sly assured Shawn and Adrian that he didn't blame them for the two women showing up like they did, and both women were able to find jobs while waiting for the Paranormal Marriage Agency to sort all this out. Beth started as a nanny for Tanya, who it seemed absolutely refused to attend school, and Jessica got a job with Lucy at the diner.

When William and Jacob found one of the missing locals in the woods, dead, things got a whole lot more serious. The man was found with his throat ripped out, but when Tyler and Max, their local morticians, did an autopsy it turned out that he had been completely drained of blood. All the signs pointed toward this being a vampire attack.

Shawn growled as he headed home from a long day of searching to no avail. They had been in the tunnels again, hoping to root out the vampire, but no luck. There was no sign of it anywhere. Even at the scene where they found the body, there had been no scent of a vampire. No scents at all.

It was worrisome on more than one level. If this vampire was that good at evading detection and had a way to stop their scent from tracing, well... things were going to get a whole hell of a lot more complicated. The vampire had to know about the wolf shifters of Devil Mountain. Vampires had stopped by the mountain occasionally in the past. After Sly and Devon mated with Chloe, the wolves were not instantly wanting to drive the vampires out. There had been a few who had stayed for some time, living on the blood that Tyler and Max were able to procure through their connections. They had all moved on, though.

Of course, there had been hostile vampires as well, but the pack had dealt with them. Now, Shawn wasn't certain if this was a single vampire or more. And why would they stick around here, when they knew they were being hunted? In his experience, most vampires didn't get a kick out of this sort of thing. Maybe they were trying out some new sort of weapon?

What was most disturbing was that Sly suspected that Jamie's incident with being creeped out that night and the other women's similar story was connected to each other and related to the vampire. Which meant that from now on, Jamie was going to stay in the cabin with him at night. No more of this hobbit hole business.

She might not like the idea, but he wasn't going to risk a vampire sneaking in without him knowing.

Shawn emerged through the trees, finding his cabin ablaze with lights pouring through the windows, even though it was just this side of dusk. Too early for a vampire to be prowling, which was why he had headed home at this time. He frowned at the cabin, noting that the hobbit hole was dark. Why would Jamie have gone to the cabin, especially at this time of day?

He yanked on clothes that he'd put in a box to one side of the clearing and dashed into the cabin. He flung the door open, earning a short scream. His gaze zeroed in on Jamie; she sat at the kitchen table, her hands clutching a glass bottle and her eyes wide.

Relief washed over Shawn, and he softly shut the door.

"Sorry. I didn't mean to scare you." He walked past her to retrieve a glass from the cupboard, which he filled with water. "We found one of the missing people. They were murdered."

Jamie drew in a shuddering breath.

"It's best if you stay in the cabin at night, now," Shawn continued. He emptied his glass and refilled it. "When Adrian gets here, we'll arrange the office so you can sleep there." He turned around, finding Jamie staring at him with wide, wary eyes. Irritation spiked through him, though he struggled to hold it in. It wasn't her fault that she'd been traumatized and her idea of sex screwed up. Not to mention it was kind of his fault for her thinking that things were going to happen against her will here. "That's a benefit to being mated to two wolves. Adrian and I will protect you."

Then he noticed that there was not one but three glasses in front of her. And the bottle she clutched was a highly expensive bottle of rum. His eyebrows rose as something else caught his eye. In the living room, sitting on the two armchairs, were the silicone sex dolls that belonged to him and Adrian. He blinked several times as he looked at the cheery faces and then turned back to Jamie.

"What?" he asked, completely thrown.

Her face went that cherry shade of red that he enjoyed so much. "I don't drink alone," she mumbled.

"And so you dug into my closet?" Shawn put his glass down and strode to where the dolls sat. They had been arranged as though chatting with each other, dressed in some of the clothes that he had bought for Jamie, looking for all intents and purposes like a friendly girl's night in.

Jamie pushed past him and put a glass in front of each of the dolls and then fell into the couch. She clutched the rum tightly, her embarrassed flush fading. Her cheeks were still pink, though. Her hands shook as she filled her glass a little too full and then sipped it down to a manageable level. She didn't release the rum bottle, though.

"Do you guys wear condoms?"

Shawn sniffed the air. There was too much alcohol scent for it to be just because of what he could see here. Besides, he was certain there was the scent of beer in the air. Quickly, he took the rum bottle from Jamie. "How much did you drink?"

Jamie shrugged. "Enough to ask you if you wore condoms. You know. When you are intimate with... whatever their names are."

"That is enough rum for you. Have you ever even drunk this stuff before?" Shawn pulled her glass away, holding her wrists with one hand when she protested and reached for it.

He tried to ignore the building pressure in his pants at Jamie's talk about the sex dolls—and pushed the images that came to mind away. She was clearly very drunk. The real question was should he make her throw up before putting her to bed? She was starting to tip over, her gaze somewhat unfocused.

"I'm just wondering how you clean inside of them," Jamie replied. "And what you like that you would prefer to do it to a doll rather than a real woman. I noticed that she," she pointed at the redhead, "has bite marks on her neck. Have you ever killed someone in the middle of sex?"

Shawn pulled her upright and propped pillows around. "No. I have never killed anybody during sex. As for the bite marks, I like biting. What Adrian and I like is rough, but we would never do it to another person without their permission, Jamie. You don't have to be scared of us, okay?" He shrugged, gathering the alcohol and taking it back to the kitchen, where he got another glass of water and gave it to Jamie. She held it, looking miserable. With a sigh, he went back down to one knee. "I know that I haven't exactly behaved—"

"My stepfather sometimes would come into my room at night," Jamie blurted. Tears flooded her eyes. "When he was drunk and didn't have a girlfriend he would come into my room and call me by my mother's name. I don't know if he really thought I was her or was just pretending."

Shawn froze, his eyes widening. His wolf started a low growl, but he swallowed the sound down, not wanting to scare Jamie.

"Today he called me," she continued, her voice growing smaller, "and said that I could come and get some of my mother's things. But when I got there, he said that Miranda left him and he... he..." She shuddered and Shawn's fists curled tightly while his wolf batted at his ribs. They needed to go down the mountain, find that bastard and rip his head off. Jamie whimpered, gulping down her water. "He tried to kiss me. He was drunk. But he never did that before. When he was calling me by name."

Shawn slowly took her hands in his. Her grip was crushing against his fingers. With effort, he pushed aside the thoughts of revenge and the desire to see that bastard trembling before him. Instead, he focused on the trembling woman that was here. She needed him. His wolf whimpered, just as much at a loss as he was when he came to knowing what to do here.

"What is wrong with me?" Jamie whispered brokenly. Fresh tears ran down her cheeks. "Why would he do that? Did I accidently give him signals—"

"Oh, Jamie, no." Shawn swallowed hard. His own behavior flashed through his mind, and he hated himself for what he had done. No wonder she had burst into tears like that! He couldn't even begin to understand what this would make her feel like—and it made him want to hide in shame for ever contributing to her pain. He swallowed heavily. "It's not you. Okay? Your stepfather's actions are not because of you. He raised you from a child; it's disgusting for him to look at you that way. It's him, not you."

"But it's not just him," Jamie whispered, her voice breaking and his heart breaking with it. "There have been other guys. Who said that they knew I wanted them.

They'd say things. But usually they didn't touch me. I just don't know what I do to draw them to me. Like those guys at Wanda's wedding. I was just trying to have fun and they…"

Shawn well remembered that incident. The men hadn't even been invited to the party, but they had shown up drunk and started harassing Jamie and Lucy. It only ended when him, Adrian, Sly and Devon had driven them off.

"They were being bastards," Shawn said, finally finding his voice. He spoke firmly, trying to indicate to her that it wasn't her fault. "If it wasn't you they'd have picked on someone else. It is not your fault, Jamie."

"But if I'd told someone about my stepfather… Everybody thinks that I sleep with him… If I just told what he did maybe…" She shuddered visibly. "But I was afraid that instead of stopping it would only get worse. That farm should belong to me, but he has the title to the land. If I told he'd kick me out and sell the farm and take everything that I want away from me."

"You told me," Shawn murmured, stroking her hair. She was tipping over again, despite the pillows, and so he helped her lay down, covering her with a blanket and then returning to kneel beside her. "Go to sleep, Jamie. Things won't look so bad in the morning."

Jamie's eyes closed and then struggled open again. She peered at him through wet lashes. "Do you want to fuck me?"

Hoo boy. After all that, what was he supposed to say? He hesitated a moment before sighing. "I want you to want me to fuck you. I want it to be something fun and enjoyable for you as much as it is for me and Adrian."

"Both at the same time?"

"Yeah," Shawn replied, nodding.

Jamie's eyes closed once again. "Then why did you make a bet to see which one would get me first?"

Shawn didn't answer that, nor did he have to. Jamie was sleeping soon enough. He cleaned up the cabin quietly, his

wolf alternating between growling and whimpering. His mind churned over what he had learned today... and he felt somehow both horrified and blessed that Jamie had trusted him enough to be the only one she had ever told.
What are we going to do? He frowned as he put the dolls back where they belonged. His frown deepened as the answer came to him. *Take care of Jamie.*
But he didn't know how.

CHAPTER TEN

Jamie woke feeling about as rotten as a root cellar of potatoes that had been flooded and then left for three months in the heat of summer. Her head rang hollowly as she lifted a hand to cover her eyes. Her wolf was in her chest, a little groggy and distant-feeling but there all the same. After her scare yesterday, the sensation of that wolf in her chest made her not feel so alone.

Normally when she woke, the first thing she did was inject herself with blockers but today… well, today as she lay there, feeling like she didn't want to move at all, she thought that maybe she wouldn't use the blockers at all. They were expensive, and why should she continually reject her wolf, anyway? She had spent so much of her life wishing she wasn't a shifter.

But her father was a shifter. She had gotten this wolf from him. Wasn't it a little bit like rejecting her father if she continually rejected her wolf? She'd never known him and had always been so determined to keep the farm because she wanted that connection. But her wolf was more to do with him than the land was. Land could be taken away from her. Her wolf could not.

Hesitantly she reached out, imagining that wolf standing in

front of her. Huge and white with coarse fur and dark eyes. It laid its head down on her chest, reaching for her as well. A sense of calm swept through her, despite the sense of shame and fear that still clung to her from the previous day.

Jamie rolled slightly, nearly falling out of bed. Her eyes flew open and she caught herself with a cry. Her wolf bolted upright in her chest but calmed quickly when it realized that there wasn't any danger.

But this wasn't her hobbit hole. Her brows furrowed as she slowly pushed herself up. She was laying on the couch in Shawn's cabin. Memories started to trickle back to her. She had felt so sullied and dirty after what her stepfather had done. Her stomach churned at just the thought. He hadn't put his hands on her but it hardly mattered. She had come rushing back here, not feeling safe until she was back in the cabin.

Then she had started a spiral. She felt so alone, so ashamed of herself, that she hadn't been able to stop her thoughts from spinning out of control. So she had turned to alcohol. For the first time in her life, she had used it to try to still the humiliation and dread and silence her thoughts. Now as she thought back, she was all the angrier at herself. Hadn't she made a vow long ago that she would not do what her mother did?

Was the land really worth this? As much as she wanted that farm, as much as she felt a part of her soul was tied to it... maybe it was time to let go. Maybe it was time to find something else to hold onto...

Shawn and Adrian's faces came to her mind. Their sly little smirks, the hunger in their eyes, the way they both had looked surprised and ashamed that day in the hot tub when she'd started crying. And she remembered the feeling of her wolf; she had neglected to refill her blockers that day and it had been strong in her chest. From the moment the two of them were in her sights, strong, hard-bodied, with gleaming skin and sculpted muscles, her wolf had been telling her to go to them.

Jamie could not recall a time when seeing a naked man had made her wet like that. Of course, it wasn't like she had a lot of experience to fall back on. Most situations when she had seen naked men were purely by accident and only a quick glimpse. A few times she had looked up men on the internet, but they were just soulless images. She had concluded that the male form didn't do anything for her—and neither did the female form.

But with Adrian and Shawn? Having spent time with them, seeing the way they worked with their pack and the way they'd defended her at Wanda's wedding, the way Adrian had watched after Shawn those months ago when Shawn was injured... It was like her eyes were opened when she saw them naked. For the first time, there was a soul to the body and somehow both together made her feel things she had never felt before.

Jamie knew what it was supposed to be like. She had read plenty of romance novels. But she hadn't expected it to be so... *real*. It was a physical thing, that wetness between her thighs, a tightening in her core, heat under her skin. She had been so ultra aware of everything her body did. It was so different from reading about it on a page and wondering if there was something wrong with her because she never felt that.

The unexpectedness of it combined with her wolf pawing at her chest, pushing her to kiss them, to give herself over to them in complete abandon, had been too much. She hadn't known how to handle it. Her brain had utterly short-circuited and as embarrassed as she was about crying like that, she was glad she had.

Her cheeks reddened as she recalled the question she had asked Shawn last night. *Do you want to fuck me?*

It both thrilled and frightened her that he had said yes. But only if she wanted him, too. That was something else that she was having trouble getting her head around... that maybe the two of them weren't pushing because they wanted her to say yes so they could do whatever they wanted with her but that they were drawn to her in such a way that they wanted to see her enjoy herself…

The sound of a cupboard door shutting made her jump. Slowly, Jamie pushed herself up onto her elbow and peered over the back of the couch. Adrian stood at the coffee maker, setting the pot on. His shoulders were slumped and there was something tired in his movements.

Jamie swallowed and slowly sat. She yawned, stretching her arms over her head. She was never a heavy drinker but was pleased when the usual hangover after something like that didn't make itself manifest. There was something to be said about keeping her wolf close, it seemed. It pawed at her ribs, tentatively, like a puppy in a new situation. Jamie wasn't entirely certain that she liked it but didn't try to push it away as she went into the kitchen to retrieve two mugs while Adrian watched her.

How much had Shawn told him? She bit her lip as she set the mugs down. Being closer to him like this, her wolf settled down quickly.

"So," Adrian said as he leaned against the counter. "You drank over a hundred bucks worth of rum last night."

Jamie blinked at him. "I did?"

"That was a three-hundred-dollar bottle and you drank a little more than a third." Adrian's lips curved into a smile as her jaw dropped. "From what Shawn told me, though, you were well within your rights to—"

"No." Jamie took a deep breath, found her mouth sticky and ran a little water into her mug so she could rinse her mouth out. When she was done, she shook her head. "I shouldn't have done that."

Adrian shook his head. "I'm not angry that you got into my rum."

"Even if you're not, I shouldn't have done it. Regardless of how expensive it was or if it belonged to you or me." Jamie wrapped her arms around her waist. "My mother used to do that. Use alcohol to escape her problems with my stepfather. It never helped her. I always swore I wouldn't… I don't want to become an alcoholic."

Adrian took a moment then nodded. "I can understand that. And for the record, I'm sorry. Shawn and I have been… well, let's just call it pushy. We never meant to cause you any distress, Jamie. Please believe that. There is a certain… I'm not sure how to put this."

Jamie chewed her lip as he combed his fingers through his hair. She had never seen any guy so awkward and struggling with how to word things before—she liked it. It made her feel like Adrian really cared and that he wanted to be absolutely certain that she would understand. And that he didn't want to accidently hurt or scare her.

"It's like in the hot tub," he said slowly as he took the now-brewed coffee and poured them each a mug. "When we were talking about how sexy you are and you got upset because, to you, we weren't complimenting you, we were fetishizing you."

Jamie added cream and sugar, nodding to show she followed him.

"Shawn and I have not had… proper relationships before." Adrian shrugged, his cheeks turning pink. "That's not to say we haven't had sex or flings, but it's never been a real emotional thing, you know? And so… All we really know about that sort of thing, the emotional side, is from what we've observed with others. And if you haven't noticed, there is a lot of show among us wolves. It's sometimes hard to parse out what's real and what's not."

Jamie tested the heat of her coffee and added a little milk to cool it down. Even though she wasn't entirely certain what she was meant to say to Adrian about this, her wolf snorted with happiness, its tail wagging. Certainly, she'd never known any man to be so vulnerable with her before.

Are Adrian and Shawn rare among men? Or have I just not had enough experience with them?

Shawn came padding into the kitchen, yawning as he scratched his head. He gave her a small smile and she returned it.

"Feel better?" he asked, taking Adrian's mug.

"Yes." Jamie chewed her lip and then blurted, "Thank you for not being angry last night."

Shawn leaned against the counter while Adrian fixed himself a new cup of coffee. "Why would I be angry with you?"

"I don't just mean with me," she said. "I mean in general. With the way I was feeling... I just... If you had gotten angry, then I would have had to defend him... and I didn't want to do that."

Shawn frowned heavily. "Why would you have to defend him?"

Jamie shook her head as her wolf cricked its tail in annoyance, asking the same question.

"Because no matter what he's done, he is still my stepfather. He is the only father I have known." Jamie frowned into her mug. She didn't know how to say this. "I guess... that's one reason why I never told anybody. Because I hate him, and I wish he'd die, but I kind of hate myself for wishing he'd die. Like it's my fault somehow."

Both Adrian and Shawn set down their mugs. They stepped toward her in unison and then stopped. Their expressions, hesitant and longing at the same time, made her breath catch in her throat. They stood there, as though waiting for permission. Hesitating, she nodded slowly. Together, they came forward, wrapping their arms around her together.

"It's not your fault," Adrian murmured into her hair while her wolf lay down, content.

"It's never your fault," Shawn agreed. "And whatever you feel, those feelings are valid. Understand? It can be confusing and complicated, but there is no right or wrong way to feel in this situation. You can love and hate someone at the same time. You're allowed to mourn the relationship you wish you could have had while wanting nothing to do with that person."

Jamie leaned into their embrace, feeling safer with their arms around her than she had for a long, long time. A shudder ran down her spine as emotions built and welled in her. Before she knew it, she was crying softly. They let her cry, holding her secure. Jamie absorbed their strength and let her emotions pour out of her, letting herself be utterly vulnerable and trusting them to not let her go.

CHAPTER ELEVEN

Adrian snarled under his breath as he flipped the police report shut. There had still been no sign of their elusive vampire, but yet another local had gone missing. He propped his elbows on the table, digging his hands into his hair. There was so much happening, and he didn't know what he was supposed to be doing. His wolf paced restlessly, anxious from the long days of silence.

It had been almost a week since they found that one body with indications of vampire attack. Almost a week since they moved Jamie into the cabin with them. He had brought a bunch of his stuff down from his cabin and moved into the hobbit hole for the time being. There were only two rooms in the cabin, after all, one taken by Shawn and the other taken by Jamie.

Sleep had been restless in the past week, though. When he wasn't lying awake thinking of these missing persons and trying to figure out a connection between them, he was lying awake with his cock in his hand, thinking about Jamie. Longing to put his arms around her and smother her with kisses. Longing to fill her so full that she couldn't think of anything else.

But while she was more comfortable with them now, he and Shawn had made the agreement that they would not do anything without her making the first move. Knowing more about her history made his blood boil and he wanted to rip off the heads of every man who had ever hurt her. Especially her so-called stepfather. How could a man watch a child grow up and have any sort of sexual feelings toward that child, even once they were grown? It made him sick to his stomach.

The only reason he didn't go take his rage out on the bastard was because he knew that Jamie wouldn't want him to. It would frighten her to have that much violence unleashed, especially on her behalf. She was just relaxing around them; he didn't want to do anything to make her afraid of them again.

As if on cue, Jamie padded into the kitchen, her slippered feet making soft noises. Her hair was done up in a messy bun and she smiled at him. She and the other women of the book club, including Jessica and Beth at this point, had gone up to the city today. She had come back all smiles and laughter as she told them about the fun she had had.

Casually, Adrian slid the new police folder under the other ones. He didn't want Jamie to see that there had been another person to go missing and get scared. She went to the fridge and pulled out a pitcher of orange juice and poured herself a glass. Shawn came in from outside, the inky darkness seeming to follow him in until he shut the door and light warmed the room again.

"You're in late," Jamie noted as she sat down next to Adrian. "What's up?"

"Felt like going for a run," Shawn replied. "Hmmm, orange juice."

He reached for Jamie's glass, but she pulled it out of his grasp and narrowed her eyes. "Adrian might put up with that, but I'm not going to. You want some orange juice, you can get your own."

Adrian smirked as Shawn rolled his eyes and headed for

the fridge. Just a week ago, Jamie wouldn't have been that firm nor would she have given Shawn that teasing grin. He loved to see how she was blossoming and relaxing around them. Sure, keeping it in his pants was growing more and more difficult, but even his wolf agreed, seeing her smile and laugh was better than pushing it too far and hurting her again.

Said wolf, though, didn't always know when it would be too much to push. It batted and pawed at his ribs, wanting him to go to her, sweep her into his arms and kiss her until they were both breathless. And that wasn't the only thing it wanted. He tried to tell it to be patient, but it only growled at him. It felt the draw, it could feel Jamie's wolf responding in the like and didn't understand why they weren't already naked.

Images flowed through Adrian's mind, and he let out a heavy sigh.

Only to catch Jamie's eyes flickering down to his groin where the bulge of his arousal was clear. He angled himself away to be hidden beneath the table and tried to concentrate on the police files. But he'd gone over them again and again, not finding any connection between the missing persons, and they were no distraction from the way Jamie's breath caught in her throat, the way her neck went pink, the way her teeth clenched on her bottom lip.

"Um," she said hesitantly. "There was something I wanted to... thank you for."

Shawn, unaware of Adrian's dilemma, smiled at her. "What is it?"

"Just that... you didn't make me feel like an idiot about it. And you're not... you know. Being, um... pushy."

Shawn and Adrian glanced at each other. Shawn coughed and shrugged. "It's really nothing. The most basic of respect."

"But still, thank you," Jamie pressed. "Because I know that it's not easy for you. To be patient, I mean. I know that you want... more. I just... I don't really know."

Adrian swallowed hard to try to keep his voice even, but it was still husky with desire as he asked, "Know what?"

"My... my body." Jamie's cheeks flushed red now. "I don't really understand these feelings. I've never had them before. Not even when I looked at pictures of naked men. I thought that there was something... I don't know, broken. Me being a virgin isn't just a matter of not trusting any of the guys I've known enough to sleep with them. I've never been attracted to someone else like this. It's like... I don't know."

Adrian considered a moment and leaned his elbows on his table. "When did you start being attracted to us?"

"Wellllll..." Jamie bent her head. "I mean, I've always thought you were sexy. Nice to look at. But when I started to actually feel... well, like I might want to do things with you, it was that day in the hot tub. It was like... seeing you naked... triggered something. But even then I wasn't just thinking about how nice you were to look at." She hid her face, looking so adorably embarrassed that Adrian had to smother laughter—along with pushing down his wolf who wanted her more than anything. "I kept thinking about how you looked after Shawn when he was hurt and how he had protected me against that dragon. I don't know. It was like... this is going to sound silly, but it was like I could see your souls and that was what I wanted."

Adrian's brow creased. He wasn't certain what she meant. But Shawn nodded knowingly. "Ah. So you're demisexual."

Jamie lifted her head. "What?"

"Demisexual. Unable to have a sexual attraction unless you already have a bond with someone." Shawn shrugged. "You're not going to be turned on by some random stranger; you have to know the person and like them as a person to have any attraction to them."

Jamie's eyes went even wider. "There's a name for that?"

Shawn nodded again.

"Oh."

Adrian scratched his neck, the pressure building even more in his pants. His wolf growled at him but stopped trying to push him over there, thankfully. It slunk back, pouting. He cleared his throat again. "So... did you look into getting toys so you can know what you like better?"

Jamie chewed on her thumb, her face cherry-red still, but she didn't look like she wanted to run. Yet at least. "No. I don't even know where to start," she admitted. "I wouldn't know how to use them even if I did."

"I thought you might say that," Shawn said. He grinned at her, the desire in his eyes now, too. "So, actually, I got a few things that you might want to try out. Nothing that's penetrative to start with, that might be a little too far at this point, but just some things to help you understand the way you like to be touched. If you want them. If not, I can get rid of them."

Jamie flushed an even darker red and looked away. The idea of her laying back with her legs spread out, a vibrating wand in hand, glistening as she worked herself, was too much for Adrian. He coughed, bolting upright. His pants were painfully tight, and he grabbed the police folders to hide himself from view.

"I'm going to take these back to the... the thing. In the office," he said to Shawn.

"The filing cabinet?" Shawn grinned wickedly at him, although why he was so smug when it was clear that the conversation was having an equal effect on him, Adrian didn't know. "We moved it to my bedroom, remember?"

"Right," Adrian mumbled and hurried from the room. Jamie and Shawn spoke in low voices, but he didn't listen to them. Instead, once he was in the bedroom he shut the door and leaned against it, breathing deeply to get himself under control.

He needed release. And since Jamie wasn't ready for this just yet, that meant he would have to find other avenues. His own hand didn't feel like enough, not in his current state, so when he'd filed away the folders, he strode to the closet and pulled out the two silicone dolls. As he was laying them on the bed, deciding which of the full-figured, smiling women he wanted tonight (neither looked like Jamie and he wasn't certain if that was a good thing or a bad thing), the door opened.

Adrian froze like he'd been caught with his pants open, but it was only Shawn, who let the door fall shut behind him. He glanced at the dolls and nodded, starting to strip off his clothes.

"Yeah, me too," he agreed. "Gods! I thought I was going to blow my load right there."

"Did she take the toys?" Adrian asked, aching to know.

Shawn moaned in his throat. "Yeah, she did. Oh, right." He flicked on the white noise machine by his bed and turned it up. "Promised I'd do that, so she didn't have to worry about us hearing her. So you want your own doll or to share?"

Adrian thought of how he'd want to fuck Jamie if she was in here right now. It had been a while since they'd shared a doll, but he would most certainly want to share Jamie. Maybe they ought to make sure that they still knew what to do. He ripped off his shirt, eyeing the two dolls. "Let's both have our redhead."

"Good idea. Fuck, fuck, fuck! I have never had my wolf ride me this hard," Shawn groaned as he fumbled in his nightstand for the lube. "It wants her. So bad. What the fuck are we gonna do, Adrian? How the fuck are we going to get through this?"

"Patience, I guess," Adrian grunted. He stripped off his pants, his cock springing free of its constraints. He licked his lips as he and Shawn arranged the doll onto her hands and knees, both of them kneeling on either side of her. "Jamie wanting the toys is a good start, right? Look at how much progress she's made in the last week." He took the lube, filling the doll's hole with it as he imagined Jamie on her hands and knees between them. "It won't be long now until—"

The door swung open. And Jamie stood in the doorway, one hand lifted as though she was in the process of knocking. Her gaze swept over the scene, of the doll between him and Shawn. Both of them naked, hard and erect. Preparing themselves and the doll for their pleasure.

Adrian expected her to turn and run away, out of embarrassment if nothing else. But the longer she stood there, the more apparent it became that she was not running anyway.

Then she stepped forward and he noticed that she had a pink vibrating wand in her hand. "I wanted to ask if this was supposed to go inside," she breathed.

Shawn shook his head. "Not that kind," he said in a strangled grunt. "It's meant to be used on, like, your inner thighs and against your clit and… other areas like that."

"Okay," Jamie whispered breathlessly and then. "Can I watch you?"

Adrian nearly lost it right there. He pressed himself against the doll's entrance, his whole body aflame and his wolf going crazy in his chest. "Yes," he said, his eyes trailing over her body. "Yes, you can watch us."

CHAPTER TWELVE

Her whole body was on fire.
Jamie's heart thrummed against her chest in excitement, her wolf pressing against her ribs, wanting her between Shawn and Adrian instead of that lifeless silicone. She held her breath as the desire welled up in her, but she couldn't bring herself to ask them to take her instead. It was just all so... new. She was just getting used to this whole idea, not to mention finally having a word for something she'd always thought meant she was broken. Demisexual.

Right now, her desire and lust were intricately connected to the men before her. Not just their beautiful bodies, not just the sculpted muscle, the clever smiles. But because they would deny themselves flesh and blood, warmth and real skin, just to make sure that she was comfortable before anything happened. That made her desire all the stronger, and she had to hold her breath not to burst with it.

And they delayed their gratification even longer, moving the doll out into the living room so she could sit comfortably on a chair while she watched them. Jamie changed into a nightgown and grabbed a blanket so she could take care of herself without being naked in front of them.

"Is this okay?" she asked, worried. "It's not fair that I'm not letting you see me when—"

"It's fine," Adrian said. "We want you to be comfortable."

He was holding himself. The sight along with his words made her skin flame with the desire for their hands to be on her flesh, but she held herself back. Her core was tight, the moisture building between her thighs even before Shawn handed her a bottle of lube and told her how to use it.

Jamie's hands shook slightly as she did as he said, putting a little of the slippery substance on her fingers and then reaching beneath the blanket. Both Shawn and Adrian watched the movement of the blanket as she slipped the lube over her clit. It was tight beneath her finger. Her gaze kept moving between Shawn and Adrian. Neither of them had entered the doll yet. Were they waiting for her or…?

She swallowed hard as she reached for her new wand and fumbled with it. "I didn't expect you to share a single doll," she blurted. "I thought that you'd have your own dolls in your own rooms."

Shawn gave a strangled laugh. "Why's that? You know that all your book club friends—well, except the new ones—have the same sort of arrangement. You have to know that they are all together?"

"I guess… I didn't think men would do that. Unless the woman they were with really wanted it. I thought you'd be more into the other sort of threesomes."

Adrian smirked as he pushed himself into the doll now. "We like that, too. But like we said, it's hard to find a woman who likes what we like. Two women? Even harder."

He gripped the doll's thighs as he thrust into it, his ass flexing, his muscled thighs working. His abs tightened and flexed as he thrust. His head fell back, and his eyes shut, moaning in sheer delight. The flames in Jamie's body kicked up a notch, and her mouth went dry. She'd never heard a man moan before. In the few videos she had tried to watch online, it was always the woman making the noise.

On the doll's other end, Shawn wrapped his hands into her hair, tugging fiercely as he pushed himself into its mouth. The two of them thrust in what seemed perfect time. Jamie watched, her hands clutched around the vibrator, not using it yet. Her thighs clenched together as, unbidden, the thought of what people would think if they could see her entered her mind.

A cold trickle of fear ran down her spine. Her wolf growled, nudging her gently in the ribs. Jamie closed her eyes, blocking out the sight of Shawn and Adrian's movements. But their soft moans and cries stayed in her ears, as well as the steady, wet sounds of them fucking the doll between them. Her wolf nudged her again, pressing against the coldness in her chest as though to banish it.

Jamie opened her eyes again, watching the two of them. Shawn smiled at her, but there was worry in his eyes. Adrian was slowing.

"I'm fine," she assured them, now turning on the vibrator. Those thoughts of what people would think lingered, but she pushed past them like kicking through a tangle of seaweed. "I want this. I want tonight to be about the three of us… or maybe the four of us," she added with a giggle, nodding to the doll. She slid the vibrator beneath the blanket and lightly traced its head against her thigh. "Where are you in her, anyway?" she asked Adrian.

His eyes twinkled. "Wondering if I'm fucking her ass?" he grunted, his pace picking up again. "No, not this time. But I will fuck your ass when you let me."

Jamie's insides squirmed. "So that's really possible?"

"Yeah," Adrian replied with a grunt.

They didn't speak more, their movements growing ever rougher. Jamie's breasts heaved, feeling like they were swelling beneath her nightgown. She licked her lips, trying not to let loose her own cries as she moved the vibrator about her body, watching the two of them. She skimmed it over her clit, her body shuddering inward as she did so.

It was maybe too much for that right away, but she used the lube to massage the vibrator downward, until it sat on her entrance; it felt good there, without being overpowering, so she left it while she watched.

Adrian yanked the doll's leg up, a growl in his throat. His fingers dug into its fake flesh, small indents in the silicone as claws started to form on the tips of his fingers. Shawn had the doll's hair pulled tight, his lips pulled back in a snarl as he pounded into it so quickly that Jamie nearly choked just watching. They were so… animalistic. Nothing like the romance she'd read. Hard, fast, grunting, growling. Adrian fell over the doll, his teeth sinking into her shoulder.

Jamie imagined that happening to her, and her breath caught in her throat. The tightness in her core worked its way down her womb, concentrating with the vibrations spreading through her. They pulsed out into her thighs. She clenched them tightly together, the vibrator standing upright as though she, too, had an erect cock. As she continued watching them pound and growl, tearing and biting, tingles of desire washed over her.

She wanted it to be her skin tearing beneath their claws and teeth. She wanted their fingers to be digging into her flesh. She wanted to be pounded between them, crushed with their lust until she was helpless to do anything before them. She wanted them to yank on her hair, to break her virginity in every way possible, to make her cry out with mingled pain and pleasure.

A pulse went through her, a tightness in her core, her clit throbbing with need. It was so powerful. She cried out, her whole body writhing. But she couldn't continue it. She pulled the vibrator free, pulses still shivering down her thighs. She lay there gasping, feeling Adrian and Shawn's gazes turning toward her. The dark lust in their eyes burned. Her wolf howled, all but ordering her to shed the blanket and nightdress, to offer herself up as sacrifice for their desires for her.

But it was too much. She shrank in on herself, hiding her eyes as embarrassment flooded through her. It had been little less than a week since she had thought the worst of these two and now she was wanting them to take her roughly like that?

There was something wrong with her.

"Jamie?" Adrian's voice was so gentle, so unlike the way he'd been fucking the doll. He sounded breathless, but the concern poured from him so genuinely that she lowered her hands to peer at him. He left the doll to kneel beside her. "Are you okay?"

Shawn left the doll as well, his hands ever so gentle as they stroked the hair from her face.

"I'm sorry," Jamie said miserably. Her wolf was making noises and pushing her to do something, but she didn't know what it wanted. "I didn't mean to ruin it for you."

"What happened?" Shawn asked.

Jamie chewed her lip for a moment. "I... Maybe I should just go and let you finish."

"Jamie, please," Adrian said. He caught her free hand and pressed the gentlest of kisses to it. "Was it something we did?"

"No... I just..." Jamie sighed as struggled to figure out what to share—and how much. Her wolf pushed her again and she understood. It wanted her to throw caution to the wind and just admit everything. That idea was even more terrifying than the idea of sex. But... "I was watching how rough you two are. And that you're starting to shift a little bit. With your claws and teeth like that."

Both of them looked down at their hands in surprise. The claws were still there but shank away as Jamie watched.

"And I was thinking... if it was me, it'd hurt. And I wanted it. I wanted you to hurt me like that. To pull my hair and pound into me like I had no choice in the matter." She lowered her gaze, her eyes burning as she admitted it. "And then there was this feeling... and it felt good, but all of a sudden it was like I hit a wall and I couldn't do it anymore. And then I thought... there's something wrong with me for wanting this. For switching so quickly between being afraid of you and then wanting exactly what I was afraid of."

"It's not the same," Shawn was quick to say as he cupped her face in his hand, still so gentle it hurt. "You wouldn't want a cake shoved down your throat but would want to eat it, right? It's the same thing. You're allowed to have the cravings you want, Jamie. Wanting sex, having kinks, it's not bad. There isn't anything wrong with you. In fact, I think it's healthy to explore sexual desires, just so long as everybody involved is a consenting adult."

"And as for that block," Adrian continued, "Well, there is a mental aspect to these things as well. All your life you've been shamed for sex that you didn't want nor actually have. It's only natural that it'll take time for you to work your way past something like that. Be patient with yourself." He winked at her. "If we can do it, so can you."

Jamie let out a small breath, the tightness in her chest easing. Her wolf snorted and nodded. She touched her sternum and smiled at them. "Thank you," she whispered. "I think I'm okay now. You can go ahead and finish."

Both of them smiled at her. They seemed satisfied with her response because they went back to what they were doing. Jamie didn't use the vibrator on herself again as she watched them, working in unison as they found their completion in the silicone. Heat still lingered under her skin but more than that... like when they'd both held her in their arms, a sense of peace and safety swept through her. And she knew. Maybe she wasn't ready just yet, but it wasn't going to be much longer.

Soon, she was going to have all the things she hadn't allowed herself to dream of.

She was not broken. And she was going to prove it to

herself, and her whole world was going to change even more than it already had.

CHAPTER THIRTEEN

Shawn rubbed his eyes, accepting the coffee that Adrian handed him. It had been a rather... interesting night. Shawn smirked as he drank the coffee, thinking about how much more intense the whole thing was. He hadn't touched Jamie in a sexual manner at all and yet felt deeply and profoundly satisfied with the whole thing. It had been so intimate in a way he couldn't describe, having her eyes on him while he took his pleasure. Knowing that she was getting enjoyment just from watching him. It had made him feel...

Well, he wasn't sure what the word was. But it was special. Something that he had never had before, no matter who he'd slept with in the past.

He caught Adrian's smirk and knew that his partner was thinking the same thing. For a moment they just stood there, drinking their coffee. Jamie was asleep in the office-bedroom. Shawn had peeked in on her (the door was open) before coming out to the kitchen. She slept soundly, more relaxed than he had ever seen her. The vibrator lay beside her pillow, and he'd been struck with the desire to thank it for its service the previous night. It had been the only thing besides Jamie's own hand to touch her during their sex, and he was glad that she had found so much enjoyment with it.

"Jamie wasn't spending today alone, was she?" Adrian murmured. "She was going to go spend time with Beth and Jessica at Angela's farm, right?"

Shawn nodded. "Yeah. It'll be good for her to be with other women. Stop her from psyching herself out about last night."

He didn't want to leave her and neither did his wolf. It was happy just being in the same cabin as her. It had finally gotten it through its head that Jamie wasn't ready for the things that they wanted to do with her, and they would just have to be patient. Last night had been satisfying enough for his wolf, it seemed. Shawn sighed. He wanted to stay here with her today, so they could have a normal day together without any pressure. He wanted to play board games and go for a hike and just spend time with her.

But, unfortunately, they both had work to do today. It was Adrian's day off of chores for the pack, but they had agreed without talking about it that this business with Jamie's stepfather could not go on. They might not do anything that Jamie would feel guilty about, but that didn't mean he was going to get away without answering for what he had done.

A sharp knock on the door made Shawn turn. Who was visiting them at this time of morning? He answered to find Jacob and William on the front porch. Both looked grim and… was that fear? Shawn frowned as he ushered them in. Adrian disappeared down the hall, presumably to shut Jamie's door so they didn't wake her.

"Want some coffee?" Shawn asked the two.

Jacob shook his head. He drummed his fingers restlessly on the table. "We think we know what's going on and need help to prove it."

Shawn frowned at him. "So Sly teamed us up together?" That was odd. Shawn and Adrian hadn't had much to do with the newcomers to the pack other than that one time when they went over to Lucy's place to check it out. "Why didn't he put you with Roman and Omar like usual?"

"Because Sly didn't put us on this at all," William said, his voice low and calm, but there was that same sort of restlessness in him as there was in Jacob. "Our theory sounds pretty crazy and we don't want to have Sly thinking that we're idiots when we're so new to the pack. Roman and Omar are taking Wanda to the city for some sort of OBGYN appointment."

Shawn's eyes widened. Surprise and jealousy swept through him. Soon he and Adrian were going to be the only original members of the pack who didn't have kids. And the idea of Jamie being a mother, of being a father... it did something to him that he liked. "Wanda's pregnant? But why aren't they getting Miriam to be their midwife?"

Jacob gave him an annoyed glance. "We don't know the details. Besides I think it's something to do with checking fertility. But that's not the point. The point is, they're not available to come with us, and Clinton and Trevor can't know about this. Not yet."

"Why not?" Adrian asked from behind them, having returned to the kitchen.

Jacob and William glanced at each other. William jerked his chin, telling Jacob to tell them. He sighed. "It has to do with the dragon that kept us as slaves. We need to go search his palace. We would rather not bring that up around them until it's absolutely necessary. They'll think we have to tell Lucy, and she doesn't need that stress right now."

Shawn frowned. How could this possibly be connected with that dragon? He'd been killed months ago! And he hadn't had any vampires at all.

But Adrian clapped him on the shoulder, nodding to him. He thought it was a good idea to check it out, at least. Shawn agreed but nodded. "Adrian has some business down in Deville, but I can tell Sly that we're checking something out over there without specifying why if you don't want to risk Sly getting pissed off with you."

"Thank you," Jacob murmured, a haunted look in his eyes.

"I'll wait here until Jamie wakes up," Adrian sighed. "You can go ahead. I'll get her to the other women before I do my thing."

Shawn nodded. Although he would have liked to have helped put Jamie's stepfather in his place, this was also important. The former slaves didn't like to talk about what happened to them when they were under the dragon's thumb, so for them to bring this up at all, they had to have good reason. Besides, they didn't have any other leads to go on.

Soon enough, they were at the dragon's palace. It was a hollowed-out mountain on the far side of the valley in the shadow of Devil Mountain, the unclaimed wilderness opposite from Deville. The wolves stared up at the heavy doors that had so recently been their prison with trepidation. Shawn's lip curled up in a snarl. These two had been part of the party that had attacked Jamie, which had ended with him being so terribly wounded. He had forgiven them, of course, knowing that they had little choice, especially if they wanted to protect their daughter, but he did not like the reminder of being so helpless.

"So. What are we looking for?" he asked as they entered the cold halls.

"Not sure," Jacob replied. He tried the light switch, but the lights remained off. "Generator must be dead."

Shawn grunted as he pulled a flashlight out of his pack. They had run here as wolves, but that didn't mean they didn't come prepared. He flicked it on and cast the beam down the corridor. The carpets had several months' worth of dust on them, but it didn't look like anything was disturbed.

"Lucy said that the thing she sensed that day up at her cabin reminded her of being here," William said as he got out his own flashlight. "And the dragon used to brag about how he got his 'powers' from containing a vengeful spirit, which he alone could guard the world from."

"He learned to make his potions somewhere," Jacob added, grimly.

Shawn hummed to himself as they headed down the left corridor. "A vengeful spirit, eh? Well, we have come across vampires that were able to use certain drugs and plants to zombify other vampires. The potions and magic that he had were probably some sort of unexplained science. Wouldn't surprise me if he'd gotten them from the vampires, either. They're into all sorts of fucked-up shit."

"This thing we're trying to catch is supposedly a vampire," Jacob replied, his tone dark. "And yet leaves no trace or scent behind. Sounds like some 'unexplained science' to me. It's possible that the dragon had a vampire prisoner that he got the knowledge to make potions and magic from that is now free."

Shawn shrugged. He wasn't sure he bought it, but they did have a good point.

They were halfway to the generator when they came to a giant hole in the wall. The edges were blackened, charred, dirt and rocks scattered outward and even embedded in the opposite wall. Shawn inspected it and whistled. He hadn't seen anything like this, not even when he was back in the military. As he put his hand on the edge of the hole, peering inward, a chill swept down his spine.

On the other side of the hole was… blackness. When he shone his flashlight in, the beam disappeared into nothing. There was no floor, no ceiling, just emptiness as far as their light shone.

It was more than creepy. His wolf snarled, his hair on end as it urged him to get out of this place. A sense of pure danger flooded outward from that empty hole. When he turned to look at the other wolves, they had retreated several feet. Both of them looked at him with expectant expressions.

"Okay," he admitted, "maybe there is something to your theory. But this isn't exactly proof, you know."

"It's enough to get Sly to come take a look, though," Jacob said. He edged backward. "Come on, let's get out—"

An explosion rocked the air. At least, it felt like an explosion. Shawn was picked up and thrown back. He toppled into Jacob and William, bringing them all down. Only—there was no noise. No sound of explosives going off. No burst of light and fire. Only the percussion that rammed into him.

Shawn gasped for breath, his head ringing. Shadows passed over his vision, something that was almost solid but not quite. He blinked rapidly, trying to lift himself up despite the pain that throbbed through his body.

The sound of laughter rang through the air. And it felt like everything disappeared around him. Something was stepping on him, crushing him. His wolf howled, and there was a sensation of something tearing inside of him. Like giant claws ripping into his very soul and trying to pull him apart. His chest seized, his lungs unable to draw air. He tried to scream but couldn't, locked as he was.

Then it was gone. He lay on the floor, cold seeping through his body but the warmth of Jacob and William nearby. His wolf howled even more, though, thrashing back and forth and wailing. Desperation seized him.

He knew, without word or conscious thought, that Jamie was in danger. Like a premonition, he could feel her pleading for help. But no matter how hard he fought against the encroaching darkness, it was useless. The flashlight guttered out, and he was left in the void of blackness, with only the howling of his wolf to let him know he was still alive.

CHAPTER FOURTEEN

Angela wasn't feeling up to having visitors since the twins had kept her up all night, so Jamie instead invited Beth and Jessica to Shawn's place to hang out in the hot tub. Since Jacob and William were working that day, Beth had Tanya. Shortly after they arrived and Adrian left for some business in town, Lucy had arrived to, stating that she was taking the day off of work.

Jamie was more than happy to have all the company. She was riding high on her experience with Shawn and Adrian the previous night, her whole body feeling light and airy. She couldn't remember the last time she felt this content with life. It seemed to her like nothing could go wrong. She did know, however, that if she was alone she would start thinking about things she didn't want to think about, and she really didn't want to end up feeling any sort of regret for what had happened last night.

Tanya's chatter was enough to keep her mind occupied, though. The little girl told her all about the lessons that Beth had for her and how it was easier to learn things at home than at school.

"We have agreed to have some days home-schooled," Beth said as they slung their towels over their shoulders. "And we're hoping that Tanya makes friends soon, aren't we?"

Tanya scowled at that. Jamie laughed, although she filed it away to tell Beth about her own experiences in school here. She understood the desire for Tanya to have social interactions, but it would do her no good if she was the one being picked on. Still, that was not a conversation to have in front of Tanya.

"It's just around back," she told Jessica when she queried as to where the hot tub was. "You can just put the cover to the side. I'm just going to grab some sodas for everyone and will be out."

"I'll help," Lucy volunteered.

Jamie smiled gratefully at her.

Once they were alone, though, Lucy put her hand lightly on Jamie's wrist. She felt rather cold, and Jamie gave her a quizzical look. The other wolf didn't seem to notice, though. Her brows were pinched with concern.

"Is everything okay, Jamie?"

Jamie laughed. "Yeah. Everything is great. Why?"

Lucy lowered her hand. She straightened the strap of her swimming suit, which barely contained her rather large breasts. After a moment, she sighed and looked back up at Jamie. "This has been something weighing on my mind for some time. I should have said something earlier, I know, but I just didn't want this happy ending to end up not so happy. But I know when a woman is being held against her will. So what is happening with Shawn and Adrian?"

Heat rushed to Jamie's cheeks, and she bent her head. "Nothing. I'm not being held against my will."

"Aren't you?" Lucy's tone made it clear she was not going to back down from this.

Jamie sighed. "It's complicated. My stepfather arranged all of it to start with, and I didn't have a say in the matter, no. But Adrian and Shawn have been wonderful. We've been open and talking to each other. I'm starting to get along with my world better. So, yeah. Everything is fine. Thank you for your concern, but you don't need to be worried about me."

Lucy sighed. "Are you certain?"

"Yes. More certain than I've been about anything." A wide smile spread over Jamie's face because it was true. Last night had been a huge leap forward. She knew that it was unrealistic to expect that everything was different now or that she would have no more challenges, but it truly felt like she had gotten over her biggest hurtle. Her wolf agreed, wagging its tail as she thought of Shawn and Adrian. "It's been a long time since my wolf and I were united like this. I didn't realize how much I missed her until now. And Shawn and Adrian are showing me things that I didn't think were possible. I can't tell you how much this last week has changed me. I think… I think I'm truly happy for the first time in my life."

Lucy smiled. She stroked Jamie's hair and then let out a chill little laugh. Jamie's wolf went rigid, and a cold feeling swept through her. Lucy's smile widened, becoming exaggeratedly huge with rows and rows of teeth while her form distorted, stretching and changing and darkening.

"It's such as shame, then." The voice didn't come from the mouth but rather reverberated in her mind. "To find joy only to lose it all."

A sense of something came at her, rushed through Jamie's being. Her wolf howled and snapped. She threw herself forward, her head snapping into Lucy's. Lucy reared back, letting out a surprised snarl. Jamie stumbled toward the door, her heart in her throat. The sun seemed somehow darker and colder than it had been.

"You can't escape," the voice hissed in her mind. *"They can't save you."*

Jamie cried out as something hit her, driving her to her knees. She heard a howl somewhere and her heart seized. *Adrian. Shawn.* What was happening? What was this thing? *Save me!*

CHAPTER FIFTEEN

Adrian wiped off his hands as he turned to glare down at Jamie's stepfather. The man lay prone on the ground, looking up at him with an expression that was confused, surprised and outraged all at once. His jaw hung open, his bloodshot eyes and red face showing that he hadn't sobered up much at all since Adrian arrived.

"I want you to take a good look at that," Adrian said, nodding toward the punching bag that hung split, its contents spilling everywhere. He'd punched it hard enough to split open his knuckles, but the single blow had practically made it explode. And that was after Jamie's stepfather tried to attack him and he'd easily pushed him over. "Now imagine that I punched you in the head instead."

The man looked from the punching bag back to Adrian and then once more to the punching bag.

"The only reason that I am not here to beat you to within an inch of your life," Adrian continued, tossing the bloody rag onto the man's chest, "is that Jamie would feel responsible, and I am not going to do anything that causes her distress. But just look at that. Look at it good and hard and just imagine what I will do to you if you ever hurt her again. And then think about what I might decide to do to you to make you pay for the pain you already caused her. Then remember that I'm not the only wolf shifter in Devil Mountain—and that the sheriff if part of our pack, too. Just remember that when you decide what your next move is."

Her stepfather pushed himself to a sitting position. "I never did anything to that little bitch—"

Adrian kicked him over. It took more effort not to stomp through his chest than it did to knock him back. "Think before you talk," Adrian cooed and then walked away.

Jamie didn't want them to kill him. Didn't want them to beat him up. And they would respect that... but that didn't mean that he was just going to get away with it. If he knew what was good for him, he'd be out of Deville within the day.

As Adrian was getting into his truck, though, he was suddenly hit by a gulf of fear. His skin grew cold and his wolf froze. His heart pounded as the sense that Jamie and Shawn were in trouble washed over him, like a physical sensation of bugs crawling on his skin. He was off before he even realized what he was doing; he was in the truck and hurtling back toward Shawn's cabin, his hands so tight on the steering wheel that his knuckles were white.

He arrived to everything looking still and silent, and he cursed himself. Neither Jamie nor Shawn were supposed to be here! But when he whirled the truck around, intending to go to the farm Angela owned with Tyler and Max, his wolf snapped at his throat and clawed at his chest. He continued, but it only became more frantic and he slammed on the brakes.

"They're not here," he argued, but at that moment he heard women's voices crying out.

Adrian threw the door open and dashed out. Following the sounds of the calls, he came to the hobbit hole. The door was locked, the shades drawn behind the windows. He pounded on the door, throwing all his weight on it.

"Jamie!"

"Adrian!" Relief washed over him at the sound of her voice. There were some scrambling noises from the other side of the door, and then it was thrown open.

Adrian grabbed Jamie, pulling her tight against him. His wolf still snarled and paced, anxious and fearful for Shawn. Adrian looked past Jamie, seeing Beth and Jessica huddled in the back with Tanya between them wrapped in a towel. All three of them looked terrified, looking at him as though they weren't quite sure who he was. He ignored them for now, focusing on Jamie.

"Are you okay?" he asked, cupping her face in his hands.

Jamie shuddered. "No. There was... Lucy..."

Adrian frowned. "What about Lucy?"

Jamie shuddered again. "I don't know what happened. I was talking to Lucy and she started to... Change. It was like she was something out of a nightmare! She attacked me. It felt so cold, like she was stealing the warmth from my skin... Then Tanya started screaming and Lucy disappeared. Then she was there again, and she chased us in here and she's been prowling around and laughing ever since."

Adrian clutched Jamie tighter as he looked around. There was no sign of Lucy anywhere. "Go back inside. I'll take a look around."

"But Adrian... Shawn is in danger. I can feel it, I—"

"I know." Adrian's throat tightened, but if their places were reversed, he would want Shawn to first make sure that Jamie was no longer in danger. His wolf was agitated, but he couldn't figure out what it wanted him to do. He ushered Jamie back inside the hobbit hole and had them lock the door before he shifted forms.

There was no sign of Lucy. No prints, no scents, nothing. He could smell Jamie, Tanya, Beth and Jessica but Lucy? No. If Jamie hadn't said something, he never would have thought she was there.

Just like the attacks that had been happening around

Deville.

A howl burst from his throat as two wolves emerged from the trees. He attacked, snarling fiercely; but when his teeth bit into the shoulder of the one nearest and he tasted blood, he knew in his gut that these weren't phantoms. He backed off and shifted back to human form, holding his hands out in a peace gesture.

"What the fuck, man?" Clinton shouted at him as he shifted to human form as well.

Trever followed suit, clutching his bleeding shoulder.

"We were attacked," Adrian explained. "What are you two doing here?"

"Looking for Jacob and William. We got a message saying they were checking something out with you guys." Clinton glared at him, not ready to forgive, but Trevor straightened and dropped his hand. Blood smeared his tattooed skin, but he would heal soon enough.

"They were headed to the dragon's old palace," Adrian grunted. "I had business in town. Any idea why they'd go there?"

Clinton and Trevor both looked at a loss. Adrian led them back to the hobbit hole after they put on pants and brought the women out again. Tanya ran to her 'uncles', sobbing out incomprehensive words. They hugged her tightly as Jamie quickly explained what happened. By the time she was done, Tanya had stopped sobbing, instead curling up against Clinton as she trembled violently. Adrian flinched as he looked at her; how much more terrifying would all of this be to her? For her aunt to be acting like that…

"I didn't find any trace of Lucy around here," he said pushing aside his empathy. It wasn't going to help them figure out what was going on here, nor would it help Shawn. He had to be cold, to look at nothing but facts and not feel this increasing panic in his chest. "Not even her scent."

Clinton and Trevor both frowned, confused and mystified.

They glanced at each other while Beth and Jessica looked around nervously.

"Well?" Adrian snapped at the two other wolves. "Do you have any idea what this could be? Jacob and William thought it was coming from the dragon's palace."

"I don't know," Clinton said, shaking his head. "I don't know why they would go back there at all! How could any of this have something to do with him? He's dead! And what would that have to do with Lucy? She wouldn't go around attacking people, and she's not some shape-shifting monster."

Trevor nodded his agreement. "We have known her since we were kids. She practically raised us! She's a normal wolf just like—"

Beth suddenly let out a high-pitched scream. Adrian jumped, whirling to face the new threat. Lucy stood on the edge of the clearing, arms wrapped around herself. Eyes wide, skin pale. Adrian snarled, pushing Jamie behind himself.

A dark shadow loomed behind her, black vines wrapping around her. Beth screamed again as Lucy's hands stretched out toward them, a cry on her lips.

"Help me!"

Clinton and Trevor both lunged forward, Clinton trying to pass Tanya to Beth as he did so. Adrian grabbed the both of them and yanked them back. When they snarled and turned on him, he shoved them toward the hobbit hole. Beth snatched Tanya and ran in, Jessica close behind her. Jamie's fingers dug into Adrian's arms.

"We know you're not Lucy," he snarled, his wolf howling. A bitter taste crept up his throat, and he hoped he was right. "What have you done with her?"

"Help," Lucy cried again.

Clinton punched Adrian hard in the face. Jamie let out a sharp yelp as darkness and pain exploded over his vision. He stumbled, his wolf howling a warning. A growl built in his chest and he leapt forward, his hands grasping blindly.

He grabbed one of them, he didn't know which and spun on instinct. A fist whistled by his ear as he yanked his target off-balance. Another howl burst from behind him.

Then the air went cold and dark as laughter filled the clearing. The man he grappled with stopped his struggling long enough for Adrian to look over, to see Trevor on his knees before Lucy. The darkness had disappeared, and she had him by the throat, a wicked gleam in her eyes as she laughed all the louder. Her mouth stretched out, impossibly large just as Jamie had described.

Only there weren't rows of teeth in that mouth. They were rows of fangs—vampire fangs.

Adrian and Clinton threw themselves forward together. Their fists landed on Lucy in the same instant—only there was nothing for their fists to meet. Adrian yelped as his fist passed through air, Lucy's image having vanished in the blink of an eye. That same laughter rang horrible. The sensation of bugs on his skin was back, a thousand tiny insects with hook-like feet burrowing into him, latching on. Draining him of energy the way a vampire drained their victim of blood.

"No!" He heard the cry somewhere behind him even as the cold invaded his blood, driving him to his knees.

"Don't," he choked out, knowing it was Jamie, knowing that the howl that followed was her shifting forms.

He forced himself back to his feet, his wolf snarling as it surged forward. The presence around him felt cold and empty—but formless. Like how his wolf felt, only this was cold, unbound, without edges or borders. He threw his head back, howling as he stretched his arms out, grabbing onto the darkness the way he would hold his wolf. His wolf lurched, as though lunging from his chest, and snapped its jaws around the darkness. Together they yanked hard against it.

The cold laughter was replaced by a hideous screech. Adrian held fast, not even knowing what he was doing—

And then Jamie was there.

Her white wolf leapt into the darkness, biting and snapping as though she could tear it apart like a physical thing. Adrian's concentration broke as he reached for her, tried to warn her. But it was too late. The dark wrapped around her; the laughter was back. And then the dark and Jamie both disappeared.

He stood there, heart pounding, arms still outstretched. His mind tumbled over what had happened, unable to accept that Jamie was just… gone. His wolf howled, panic clawing at his chest.

Adrian surged to his feet. "You," he roared, flinging his hand out. He pointed at Beth, standing in the doorway of the hobbit hole with Tanya clinging to her. "Call Sly and tell him we're heading to the dragon's palace. The whole pack needs to come. And you," he pointed at Clinton and Trevor, both of whom were on the ground, gasping and clutching at their chests, "you're with me."

He shifted back to wolf form, throwing himself toward the trees. It couldn't be coincidence that this happened just when Shawn and the others went to the dragon's old palace. He was going to find out what was going on, and he was going to stop it. He was going to get Jamie back— no matter what it took.

CHAPTER SIXTEEN

Shawn groaned, consciousness tickling at the corners of his mind. He lifted one trembling hand—or at least he thought he did. His body felt vague, distant. Almost like he was floating on a river, getting farther and farther from the anchor of his physical form. Somewhere in the distance a wolf was howling. He wished it would be quiet. He reached for his own wolf, needing to feel its comforting presence.

But it wasn't there.

A ripping, tearing feeling washed through his consciousness. A grunt and groan echoed from his throat as everything sort of contracted inward. There was no pain, no feeling of physical body, and yet agony washed through him. He felt like he was being stretched in two directions, like his human form and his wolf form were being torn apart from one another. The fear was unbearable, and he let out a howl.

Suddenly he jerked upright, back in his body, his skin flaming and tingling. His wolf latched onto one of his ribs as it panted, shaking in his chest. His breath came rapidly while his heart jerked all around in his chest. The echo of pain lingered through his form, and he was uncertain if it was physical or something else.

Hands grabbed his shoulders and he yelped, but Adrian's voice was there, calming him. "I've got you! I've got you. Breathe, Shawn."

Shawn focused on his lungs, forcing them to draw in breath. Slowly he calmed. His vision slid into focus to find Adrian right in front of him. Fear and relief were mingled in his partner's eyes.

But Shawn's own relief was short-lived. "Jamie!"

"I know," Adrian murmured, something tightening in his gaze. "Can you get up?"

Shawn grunted in annoyance at the presumption of his weakness. He staggered to his feet, his head spinning as he did so but not so bad that he couldn't keep his balance. Clinton and Trevor were helping Jacob and William get to their feet as well. All four of them looked flat-out terrified, but Shawn didn't have any brain space to waste on that.

"Jamie's in danger," Shawn said, pushing Adrian off him. "You have to go home and—"

"I was home. Something took her." Adrian's gaze blazed with fear, hatred and determination. "It's connected with this place. She's nearby; I know she is. But I can't save her by myself, Shawn. I need you."

Shawn's wolf snarled and barked. It still felt weak, almost like he had been on blockers, but it was still raring to go. He shoved aside his own weakness and pushed off the wall. His knees trembled, and he bit back a curse as he fell back into the wall. What was his fucking body doing? He didn't have time to feel weak and helpless, not when Jamie was in danger!

"It's Lucy," Clinton blurted.

"What?" Jacob snapped.

"Lucy attacked us," Clinton continued. "At Shawn's place. Only it wasn't… it wasn't Lucy. It was nothing like her. But it looked like her. Maybe it took her… if it's the vengeful spirit the dragon always talked about, maybe it broke free and inhabited Lucy. Or maybe it was in her all

this time and the dragon used his potions to subdue it…"
Shawn pushed off the wall again, his chest feeling tight as his wolf snarled ever louder. "It doesn't matter what it is! It's got Jamie! We have to find it… find her… get her back."
Adrian grabbed his arm as he stepped forward. Shawn would have snarled at him, but his legs gave out again and he had to sag against Adrian. Anger built ever stronger in Shawn fueled by fear. They didn't have time for any of this! Adrian should just leave him here, go find Jamie and save her before whatever this thing was could hurt her. He could almost hear her calling his name, even now.
"Don't you think I want to go charging after her?" Adrian snarled as though he could read Shawn's mind. "But that thing just wrapped around her, and they both disappeared. We need more information if we're even going to find where she is! It's connected to this place; I know it is. You four," he barked, turning back to the dragon's former slaves. "What did the dragon say about this spirit thing? I need details!"
Jacob screwed his eyes shut. He was standing without any support and Shawn snarled under his breath, furious at his body for being so weak.
"He said he found it when he was travelling in Europe. He subdued it and brought it back here to lock it away. He said he was protecting the world from it and we'd see what dangers really lurked in the world if we ever killed him. I never believed it, though. Not until now."
"And this attack on you here. Where did it come from?" Adrian pressed.
"There," Shawn growled, gesturing to the hole in the wall. Only it wasn't there. The stone was smooth, no sign of burnt edges or blasted hole left behind. He stopped, eyes going wide. Was his mind playing tricks on him now? "There was a hole! An explosion… what the fuck is happening?"
Adrian growled as he tugged Shawn with him, heading

down the corridor with the other wolves following. "I have an idea about that. The attacks were vampiric but with no sign of a vampire left behind. And that thing that looked like Lucy was immaterial. It stuck to the shadows, avoiding direct sunlight. Where did vampires even come from? They take such different forms in various cultures and quite often take the form of spirits."

Shawn frowned. His legs weren't so shaky now and he was able to stop leaning on Adrian. His wolf pressed him hard down the corridor and as they went into the darkness, the imagined voice of Jamie became clearer.

"I think this thing, whatever it is, is an early form of vampire. Trapped without a true form," Adrian continued. "And I think it's trying to steal our forms. When it attacked, it felt like something was trying to take my human form from me—"

"Me too," the others said, almost in unison.

"Like it was trying to rip me into two forms," Jacob murmured.

A chill ran down Shawn's spine. They came to the spot where the hole had been, and he stopped. Adrian reached to pull him, but Shawn shook him off. He could almost feel Jamie's wolf howling. His mind whirled. If this thing was a spirit without form, if it was looking to pull their forms apart…

"It wants physical form," he murmured in understanding. "It wants to rip us in half, to steal our human form. And that's why it took Jamie. Because she has always fought against her wolf. They're disconnected already."

"And why we need to keep going, so we can find her," Adrian insisted.

But Shawn sucked in a deep breath. He didn't know what happened at the cabin, but if it had looked like Lucy then they couldn't exactly trust their eyes, could they? He closed his eyes. There had been a hole here. And there still was, he knew there had to be. The image of the dark emptiness made a chill run down his spine, but he pushed it forward.

His wolf howled, feeling Jamie so close…
Shawn strode forward, into the wall.
Only he didn't hit solid stone. Nor did the floor fall out from under him. The other wolves shouted behind him in surprise. When he opened his eyes, he found himself in a dark, dull chamber. A bench was the only thing in the room, a skeleton laid out across it. And by the skeleton…
"Jamie!" He rushed forward.
Jamie lay limp, her skin pale and her eyes closed. He dropped to his knees beside her, drawing her into his arms. Her breathing was shallow and when he checked for her pulse, it was almost non-existent. Terror ripped through him as his wolf whimpered and whined. He held her tight, as though he could give her his warmth and bring her back. When he turned, he found the other five stumbling through the hole in the wall that was now perfectly visible. His gaze sought out Adrian, who had stopped in the doorway, his eyes wide, one hand reached out but otherwise frozen.
"Help her," Shawn pleaded. He didn't know what to do. But Adrian always had the answers.
But from the look on his face, Shawn knew that this time, Adrian had no answers. He met Shawn's eyes, desperation and hopelessness in his gaze. It seemed that all time had paused and yet sped at the same time, Jamie's form growing colder in his arms even as his own heartbeat slowed.
Jacob and William were suddenly there. They pulled Jamie away from Shawn. He yelped, then snarled. Adrian surged forward, but Clinton and Trevor held them both back. Shawn shouted, fighting against Clinton. Jamie needed him! They couldn't do this, couldn't keep them apart.
"She was hit over the head," Jacob murmured as his fingers probed her skull. "Concussion, probably."
William grunted, patting his hands down Jamie's body. Adrian and Shawn both snarled at the same time, but Clinton and Trevor shoved them back.

"They were paramedics," Clinton shouted in Shawn's face. "Calm the fuck down and let them do their job!"

Shawn realized that his fingernails had started to turn into claws. He didn't like the look of William's hands on Jamie's body, but on closer inspection, he wasn't groping her at all—he was checking for broken bones. With effort and trying to reassure his wolf, he forced himself to stop fighting to go over there and rip their fucking heads off.

They're trying to help her, he told himself. Anxiousness surged again as he held his breath. He'd received first-aid training back when they were part of the military, but he didn't know enough to actually help.

"We need to stabilize her neck before moving her. And that means no picking her up," William said, shooting a glare at Shawn. "I know you're worried, but if she has a neck injury moving her is only going to make it worse."

"She's not bleeding except from this small abrasion on her head," Jacob said. He checked her pulse. "A little slow but steady. Give us your shirts, we have to keep her warm."

Shawn had no shirt to give, having only brought pants to wear on this excursion. Clinton had a shirt that he pulled off and Adrian also was able to give one, but that was it. And Shawn automatically knew it wasn't going to be enough. He whirled to Adrian and grabbed his wrist.

"If that thing was taking Lucy's image it might mean that it's stealing her form. You have to go check it out. We can't move Jamie, and it's too cold to leave her alone. So I'll stay. I'll keep her warm. You go stop that thing."

Adrian stared at him, face pale. "I don't know how."

Shawn snorted and gave him a weak smirk. "You're a smartass, you'll figure it out. Now go! She won't be safe until that thing it locked away again. Somehow. Now go!"

He pulled off his pants to lay over Jamie and shifted to his wolf form. He gingerly lowered himself over her, covering her body with his own. She let out a soft sigh, moving ever so slightly. His wolf whined again. Shawn didn't look after Adrian as he took off with Clinton and Trevor at his heels.

William and Jacob put together a makeshift neck brace and told Shawn what to do if she started to wake up, and then they took off as well.

The cold seeped in from the dark walls as Shawn stretched there, trying to give Jamie all his warmth. His heart was in his throat, his wolf torn between wanting to stay here and to go after Adrian, to put the danger in the ground.

This is the most pressing matter, he told it firmly. Jamie was breathing, but she was not out of the woods. His gaze moved to the skeleton stretched out on the bench above them. A shudder ran down his spin as the grinning skull seemed to laugh at him. Vampire fangs emerged from the upper jaw, the whole thing perfectly articulated—like a university specimen.

A chill rolled down his spine as he saw holes drilled into the bone, wires keeping it together. It *was* a university specimen... what the fuck was going on here?

CHAPTER SEVENTEEN

Adrian's wolf growled and snapped and paced. It was difficult, keeping himself moving forward when he wanted to turn around and rush back to Jamie, to carry her out of that cold, dark hole—he didn't even know how it had been hidden like that—and back to somewhere he could make sure she was going to be okay. But he felt in his bones that she was not going to wake until they had found a way to capture that thing, that vampiric spirit.

But how?

His mind kept shooting back to the skeleton in the hole where they'd found Jamie. There was something about the whole thing that felt off, that was just... strange.

Like it had been arranged there, he thought as he and the other wolves drew closer to Lucy's cabin. *Like Jamie wasn't the true target but was only distracting us.*

A woman's scream pierced through air. Adrian shoved his thoughts aside, letting his subconscious mull them over as he burst through the clearing where Lucy's cabin was. A wolf lay stretched out in the single patch of sunlight in the densely treed area, sides heaving and tongue lolling. Stiff, eyes glazed. Like Shawn had been when they found him.

Lucy's wolf form.

And her human form was at the porch, arms clasped around Beth as she pushed Beth down. Blood dribbled down Lucy's chin, vampire fangs flashing in her mouth.

Adrian sprang forward, a snarl ripping through his throat. Lucy yanked Beth up, putting a knife to her throat. Adrian stopped while the other four crowded around Lucy's wolf form, growling and whimpering. Beth sobbed, one hand pressed to her neck where blood dribbled from two perfect holes.

That scent of rot and death that Adrian associated with all vampires except Chloe stung his nose. He growled softly, the hairs on his neck standing upright. This was no longer some spirit they were dealing with. It had taken flesh and blood—Lucy. But she still flickered at the edges. So maybe it hadn't fully taken Lucy's form yet?

"Now, now," the vampire purred. "These women long to be free of their bonds. They wish they could be far, far away, just like me. Don't stop me from giving them what we all want. Your little white wolf will live if I am able to sate myself on these others. But she'll die if you stop me from receiving my energy from other places."

Adrian shifted back to human form. He stood there, glaring at the vampire in Lucy's stolen form. Even as he watched, it seemed she was getting ever more solid. He knew it was lying. Jamie would die so long as it possessed this form. But if they killed it… he knew that Lucy would die. If the others figured it out, then they'd stop him from doing what was necessary if it came to that—

Stop, he told himself firmly. *You're smarter than this. It is not going to win.*

He paced to one side, peering intently at Lucy's form. The knife still at Beth's throat, but there was a good distance from her skin to the blade. A bluff? The vampire didn't want to lose her blood.

"You have to know that we will all die before letting you get away with this," he said slowly. "And before you simply wrapped up Jamie and disappeared or hid the wall. So why not play more tricks on our minds, huh? Why not just disappear so you can finish off Beth somewhere else?" Beth whimpered, but he ignored her.

The vampire grinned, but this was a normal grin. "You are a silly pup, aren't you? I have watched this world for a million years. You can try to kill this form, but what difference will it make? I will find another one. There are so very many people in this place who wish to leave."

"Ahhh, so that's it." Adrian stopped his pacing. A slow smirk spread over his face. He wasn't certain if he was right at all, but his muscles bunched. If he was right… then he had only one chance at this. "All the people who have gone missing. You were trying to take their forms. But you couldn't. They fought you too hard. So you killed them. Used their deaths to give yourself more energy. You can only attack people who wish to leave, though. You can only align yourself with people who have similar wants as you. Jamie's schism with her wolf allowed you to tap into her energy. Because you don't have a firm hold on Lucy's form, do you? She's still fighting you. She and her wolf both."

"The hose is almost dead. It won't be long now."

"The skeleton," Adrian murmured. "It wasn't the bones of a long-dead person. The dragon didn't have the palace long enough for a skeleton to become that clean or stay that pristine in those conditions. That was the form you were held in, wasn't it? You tried to steal his form, but he shoved you in that skeleton… was it his death that allowed your escape, then? Or was it because the skeleton itself broke?"

The vampire started to laugh but not before surprise flashed through her eyes. It was all that Adrian needed. He turned his back on Beth's pleading gaze, turning to the four wolves who gathered around Lucy's form. The last hiker they'd found had had his throat torn out. It had been drinking blood before it latched onto Lucy's form. And if blood made it stronger…

"Feed her your blood," Adrian ordered. "She's turning vampire, too. We strengthen her, then this 'vengeful spirit' will grow weaker."

There was no time for arguing, no time for the baffled expressions of the former slaves to change. Because just as he had hoped, a furious shriek split the air. He whirled around, his hand snapping up. He judged the distance perfectly and then caught the knife that the vampire had hurled at him. Beth was still in its clutches but the blade no longer at her throat.

Adrian sprang forward, shifting into his wolf form as he did so. The vampire yanked Beth's head back, but before it could bite her again, he'd bowled into them. Beth screamed and the vampire lashed out, claws striking through Adrian's thick fur. Pain burst through his skin, but he twisted, grabbing Beth in his jaws. He tossed her over his shoulder, ignoring her scream as she tumbled off the porch.

The vampire grappled with him as he pressed his paw against her head, forcing her face into the wooden planks, her snapping jaws and the deadly venom coating them facing away from him. He seized her shoulder, sinking his fangs in deeply, and shook his body. Flesh tore, making the vampire scream—and Lucy howl. He bit again and again as the vampire shrieked and kicked and clawed at him.

But it was physical now and limited in what it could do.

He pulled back, grabbing it by its leg. Snarling, he dragged her off the porch, whipping her around one way and then the other. Adrenaline poured through his own being and he knew it had to be for her as well.

He flung Lucy's stolen form close to where the other wolves were all feeding her wolf form their blood. Lucy staggered to her feet. Her wolf lunged, its jaws closing around the vampire's arm. A soul-chilling shriek filled the air. The sound of thunder and a flash of light burst from where they touched. An explosion rippled out from them, lifting all of the wolves off their feet. Adrian slammed into the porch, dropping to the ground as pain blinded him.

When he lifted his head, Lucy lay in a half-shifted form in the sunlight. She panted, her hands digging into the ground. And he grinned; vampire venom could block a shifter from their wolf form, but adrenaline counter-acted those effects. And it seemed that he had injured the vampire enough to push enough adrenaline into its system for Lucy to finally fight it off, like a virus.

Beth scrambled to her feet. She looked around wildly, shaking hard. Adrian shifted back to his human form and reached to steady her.

"Don't worry," he told her. "It can't take your body. It needs a form without a soul already attached to it. That's why it chose shifters. Why it chose Lucy. Because we have two bodies with one soul, and it could force our souls into one form and take the other."

"But," Beth started.

Jacob interrupted, rushing over to grab Beth by the shoulders, William right behind him. "Where's Tanya?"

"Tanya?" Beth's eyes widened.

"Yes!" William grabbed her as well. "Where is our daughter?"

Beth shook her head. "I told her to hide in the closet. I felt cold and I thought it was coming back. So I told her to hide. Jessica lit a bunch of candles and was doing something, but I… I was suddenly so cold. I couldn't breathe. Then Lucy grabbed me—"

"It wasn't her," Adrian reassured her. His wolf pressed against his ribs, wanting him to leave this and rush back to Jamie. His muscles trembled and the chill air made goosebumps rise on his naked skin. "It was that vampire-spirit. It brought you here to strengthen itself. My guess is that the further it got from Lucy the less control it had on her physical form because it was trying to drag itself back to her. That's why it brought you here to feed on you because it had to be close enough to gain its strength and gain full form. We stopped it, don't worry."

"Where did you leave Tanya?" Jacob asked impatiently.

Beth opened and closed her mouth. Finally she shook her head. "We were at your place. Jessica didn't want to stay at Shawn's cabin."

William grunted and hit Jacob's arm. They shifted and dashed into the trees without a word, presumably heading home to check on their daughter. Clinton and Trevor helped Lucy up and brought her to the house. She shuddered and shivered, looking pale and weak.

A hand tugged Adrian's sleeve, and he turned back to Beth. His wolf was growing ever more impatient, wanting to leave.

"Where is it now?" Beth whispered, her eyes full of terror.

Dread welled in Adrian. Of course. If it wasn't able to steal Lucy's physical body—

And he realized that his wolf felt distant. That its growls and howls were hollow in his chest. The sound of laughter filled his ears and he heard a cold voice whisper in his ear. *You think you're clever, but I don't need someone who wishes to leave this place to take their form. Say goodbye, Shifter. Your form is pleasing enough for my purposes.*

Then the feeling like a white-hot knife sliced through him. His wolf yelped as a tearing sensation filled him. Adrian let out a cry of pain as he doubled over. The only thing to flash through his mind was that the vampire needed physical form. He could feel it shoving itself into his human form, ripping his wolf way, pushing him to the wolf's body.

No!

With all his effort, he threw himself toward his wolf. He let it take over, dashing away from the others as they drew back. The forest was a blur about him as he wrestled with the formless thing that was trying to tear apart his soul. Growls ripped through his body, the cold dark sending tendrils around him like ropes.

He didn't know how he got to Shawn's cabin but suddenly found himself on his hands and knees in the bedroom. Sweat dripped down his skin as a grin crossed his face. His wolf had known what to do, too. He ground his teeth together as he pushed to his feet and yanked open the closet door.

The two silicone sex dolls tumbled out. He grabbed one, feeling its soft body beneath his fingers. The vampire's spirit still battled him, but he closed his eyes. He could almost see it, formless against his own formless soul. But he drew himself together, reaching out to snag the vampire. He pushed hard, tearing it from his body and into the silicone body he pinned.

Everything stopped. Pain ached through him, but his wolf pressed against his ribs, panting for breath as he collapsed over the doll. He panted—then felt it moving beneath him. His head jerked up as the doll bent its head. Fangs sprouted from its mouth.

Adrian flung himself to one side. It kicked and reached its fingers toward his throat. But it was too slow. Adrian snatched a rope from the closet and caught its hands. He flipped it onto its stomach and had the silicone form trussed up within seconds.

"Now you've got a physical form again," he taunted as the vampire's mouth opened and closed, but there were no vocal chords for it to speak. "And this one is going to last a long, long time."

CHAPTER EIGHTEEN

Jamie didn't know how it worked, but once the vampire's spirit was in a full physical form, it was stuck there until it was no longer suitable it seemed. On closer inspection of the skeleton in the dragon's palace, they found that its ribs had been smashed open with a large rock. Adrian guessed that the vampire had broken its physical host just enough to escape its confines and then had been building power and waiting until the dragon died. The dragon had known how to stop it, after all, and after his death, the vampire thought it was home free. But it was still bound somewhat to the physical remains it had in the palace until it could get a new one.

They sealed the possessed doll in an airtight coffin, within a temperature-controlled vault that Theron, another of the pack, designed for several million dollars. It drew its energy from a thermal source, meaning that it was constantly replenishing itself. It would be many, many years before that doll was in conditions where it would break down enough to free the vampire again.

"But how did you know you could force it into the doll?" Jamie asked several days after the doll had been buried. She lay between Adrian and Shawn in bed, their warm bodies pressed against her. Physical recovery had been quick but emotionally… well, that was going to take some time.

"I didn't know for certain." Adrian shrugged. "I picked up on the clues subconsciously I suppose. I had to stop it. All I know is that I was never going to let it hurt you again."

Jamie smiled, running her hand along his chest. The whole ordeal had been terrifying. After the spirit had whisked her away, she hadn't been aware of anything, only her wolf. They'd clung to each other, calling for her mates. "I knew that you'd save me."

Shawn kissed her shoulder, sending pleasant sparks under her skin. "Let's not talk about this anymore. It's over and everyone is going to be okay now. Beth wasn't hit by enough venom to turn her, and Lucy is slowly getting back to herself. Everybody is going to be fine. I don't want to let that thing control any more of our lives."

Jamie turned to him and stroked his hair. "I understand. We're safe and that's what matters."

She kissed him lightly. Her wolf whined playfully, tail wagging as it urged her to do more than just light kisses. And so she did. Thrills shot through her as she was able to embrace her own desires. To know that she was safe with these two, that she never had to worry about what they would think or if they would treat her badly for having sexual desires in the first place.

With everything that had happened with the vampire, it seemed almost surreal that this could still be something that burned through her. Wasn't being attacked by a vengeful spirit the sort of thing that should leave her traumatized? And maybe she was, but the spirit felt more like a bad dream than anything else.

The truth of the matter was, while it had been terrifying, it had also cemented in Jamie's mind and heart that Shawn and Adrian were her mates. Not just promised mates. It wasn't her stepfather's choice; it wasn't him getting rid of her.

No. They were her fated mates. She belonged to them, and she was happy to be theirs. They would protect her, love her, and she never had to be ashamed of her own sexuality again.

Adrian started to kiss her neck while Shawn returned her eager kisses and fireworks built under Jamie's skin. She moaned lightly and was rewarded by feeling both her mates harden against her. She could feel them tensing, trembling with desire. It made desire flow through her as well.

"Sorry that you lost your doll, though," she moaned as Shawn bent, kissing down her chest.

"Why would we care about that when we have you?" Adrian whispered huskily in her ear.

Almost in unison, they stopped. Jamie bit back on her protest as they eased back, giving her more space. But this was something they needed to talk about. After all the difficulties they'd had before and how she'd yelled at them on more than one occasion about not making the choice for her…

"Do you want to be our doll?" Shawn asked, his hand resting lightly just under her breast.

"Yes," Jamie replied. She slid her hands down their bodies, finding their cocks through their jeans. She massaged them, a thrill running through her at the solid feel against her palms. "I want to be your doll. I want you to treat me like that."

Both of them grinned in unison. They returned to kissing her fiercely, the sheer desire nearly overwhelming her. But she matched their passion with her own. She might not know exactly what she was doing, but she didn't care. She whispered in their ears what she wanted them to do to her, how she wanted them to take her virginity. They agreed and told her to pick a safe word, just in case things got too rough for her.

"Um… laptop," she said, blurting out the only thing she could think of.

Shawn nodded. "Okay. Laptop it is. We're going to tie you up and blindfold you now." He kissed her again and laughed as he drew his hand over her belly. "Who knew that our innocent little rose had such a kinky mind?"

Jamie laughed. The truth was, she hadn't allowed herself many sexual fantasies. Always was careful, as though what was going on in her mind would somehow make people treat her differently. Or maybe it was that there was just too much of a threat of her control being taken away in her daily life... but here, as Adrian and Shawn kissed her and stroked her skin as they tied her spread-eagle to the bed, their touch so gentle it hurt, she had no fear. They would not hurt her. And sure she was being tied up and they could fuck her whatever way they wanted...

At the end of the day, though, this was her fantasy they were fulfilling. They liked it, yes, but with a word she could make them stop. So she was giving control over to them, being tied in place and her clothing stripped off, her body vulnerable before them... but in actuality, she was still in control.

Adrian got a sleeping mask out and kissed each of her eyes before sliding it into place. The sensation of his and Shawn's hands on her body made her shiver, warm sparks firing beneath her skin. Nerves beat with her excitement and she giggled, her cheeks blushing as she imagined what they would look like. Then they withdrew and the noise ceased entirely.

Jamie frowned. "Adrian? Shawn?"

"We're here," Adrian called from the foot of the bed. "We're just deciding what to do with you now. We can't just shove in, you know."

Jamie wiggled impatiently. "Why not?"

Shawn laughed, more distant than Adrian. Where was he? "You told us that you wanted to be tied up and blindfolded. If you don't like what we have for you, just use your safe word."

She pouted, not liking that option at all. Moments later,

though, their hands returned to her body. It was unexpected and made her jump but as the sparks built again and their fingers coasted up her thighs and around her breasts, she relaxed back into the bed.

Lips pressed against her ribs, and hot breath wafted over her thighs. Jamie's core clenched, her breath catching in her throat. She didn't know which one of her mates was where as one of them licked her nipples and blew on them, the cold air making them stand up. The other one kissed up her thigh, strong hands opening her up. Her clit was soft beneath his tongue, but the friction still made her gasp, lifting her hips.

One set of hands held her down, the other spreading her legs further open. Jamie pulled against the ropes, imagining what sort of surprise her mates would get if she was able to rip them free. Break the bed and—

The tongue moved up her again, long and slow, while her other mate suckled at her breast. Something tightened, pulling between her core and her breasts. Her clit throbbed as it hardened, becoming increasingly sensitive the more attention was payed to it. A tightness built in her thighs, creeping up her belly. Jamie moaned as she tried to press her thighs shut, to protect herself from the increasing pleasure. Her mates held her firmly in place, and she let out a cry of mingled pleasure and frustration.

The tongue moved from the top down, causing her to jump again. But no... the other set of lips worked on the sensitive skin of her thigh now. So the one who had been kissing her breasts must have moved down to her clit.

"Eugh!" she cried out, wanting to know which was which. The smell of her own arousal was matched with theirs. One of them straddled her chest, facing downward.

"Are you enjoying that?" Adrian asked her in a husky voice, but they were so close together she didn't know if he was the one over her or the one kneeling between her legs.

"Yes," Jamie panted. "Don't stop."

"Good," Shawn replied. "Do you want a cock in your mouth?"

Jamie chewed her lip, suddenly shy even though she was exposed to them. "I don't know how," she blurted.

"We'll tell you," Adrian promised. "Do you want it?"

A thumb moved in lazy circles around her clit while fingers slipped into her. Jamie cried out, bucking her hips again. Both sets of hands caught her and pushed her down while both her mates laughed. Jamie panted, her wolf howling in her chest. It didn't want to wait any longer. It wanted them inside of her, to fill her, to stretch her out. But it was too soon. Jamie licked her lips, fighting to clear her head as the pleasure only increased. She wanted them to do this to her but hadn't expected for them to ask her more questions!

"I want to make you happy," she finally said. "Please. Do to me whatever you want."

Both of them groaned at that, the sound zinging her straight to the core. The man straddling her moved up, turning around so his knees were up by her head. One hand tangled in her hair, tugging slightly, while something was slid into her hand.

"If you need us to stop, squeeze that."

Jamie squeezed it experimentally. It let out a squawking noise, one of those rubber dog toys. She laughed as she nodded. "I just wanted to know what it sounded like. I'm ready."

A hand grasped her jaw, opening her mouth to the right shape. The man slid himself into her mouth. He tasted sweet and salty, his scent filling her nostrils. Between her thighs, her other mate renewed his efforts. He slid another finger into her. It stretched her, pressure and a slight sting of pain mingled. The man who held her head moved it back and forward, giving her instruction with what to do with her lips and tongue. She could feel him harden inside of her and it sent a thrill through her.

"We're going to have to get a couple more dolls," Adrian said from somewhere, but the hands were over her ears and she still couldn't tell where he was. "A man form and another female."

What for? The question was driven from her mind as she was spread even further open. One of her mates eased himself inside of her. He stretched her more than she thought possible. A sting of pain as he withdrew made her hand flex on the dog toy, but she didn't squeeze. It took all her self-control as something cold and slippery was dribbled on her and he entered her again.

They fucked her in unison, in a perfectly matching rhythm, one in her mouth and one between her legs. The pleasure built so fast Jamie nearly choked on it. She was aware of the toy in her hand and how at any moment she was going to squeeze it without meaning to. The thought of this ending filled her with dread, and she tried to throw it away, but a hand wrapped around hers, stopping her.

Fingers worked her clit again. It didn't take long for her to fall off the cliff, landing shuddering and shaking in a stormy sea of pleasure. Adrian's deep voice grunted and growled; she felt the man between her legs climax into her and the one in her mouth quickly moved down as the other withdrew, taking her rapidly. The sounds of his groans, of their skin slapping together, it was all too much. Jamie's body pulsed again, pushing her into yet another orgasm.

After they were all done, Adrian and Shawn removed her blindfold and untied her. They cuddled her between their bodies as she gasped, her body tender and aching.

"Why do we need new dolls?" Shawn asked idly as he traced a finger down Jamie's spine. "I enjoyed that."

"I did, too." Adrian grinned as he stroked Jamie's hair. "But I've got perverted tastes. You should know that by now. I want Jamie to wear a strap-on and fuck another man."

Jamie's eyes widened even as amusement and confusion swept through her. "What's a strap-on?"

"It's a fake dick on a belt that women can wear," Adrian

replied. His finger brushed over her breast, light and wonderful. She shivered at his touch, though she couldn't picture what he was talking about. "I have other things, too, that we can only do with another few people. But I'm also insanely jealous. I think I'd kill any man who tried to put their hands on Jamie."

He nuzzled into her neck, making her shiver with delight, as Shawn huffed. "Oh, so you're going to kill me are you?"

"I meant someone besides you," Adrian snapped.

Jamie laughed as she put her hands over their mouths. "Enough, both of you. Don't start bickering. I'm not sure about this strap-on business, but I can tell you that I have other ideas for the three of us." She gazed adoringly at the two of them, feeling satisfied, safe and like she was free for the first time in her life. She brought them to her, kissing first one and then the other. As they pressed their foreheads to hers, she closed her eyes. "I love you," she whispered, and her wolf yipped for joy.

"Love you, too," they both said together.

Warmth flooded her. Everything felt good and right. She held them all the tighter, looking forward to the future with nothing but happiness and excitement.

CHAPTER NINETEEN

Shawn let his fingers drift over the marks on the wall that showed how tall Jamie was at various stages of her life. Excitement coursed through him as he imagined one day having their child standing against the wall, marking how tall they were.

He could imagine that a lot in Jamie's childhood home. When she told them about the way she would hide in the window seat during hide-and-seek with her mother, he imagined their children hiding there. When she told them about the big oak that used to grow outside her window, he imagined planting a new tree there to grow with their children.

Of course, having children wasn't going to happen right away. They had all agreed to wait a little while at least. They had to do a lot of renovations on the old farmhouse, after all, not to mention rebuild the barn and get the fields back to prosperity. Jamie's stepfather had really let the place go, and Jamie was excited to get Wanda and her mates down here to help with the new construction as soon as possible.

"And it's too late in the year to plant anything now," Jamie said, returning to the kitchen with Adrian on her heels.

Her eyes were bright, and she was literally bouncing with each step, "but next year we'll grow squash and corn and beans and peas and carrots and potatoes. A few years back I had a good rapport with a lot of the stores in the city, I'll see if I can build that back up to sell things to them again. And it'll be a few years before we can sell as organic since you-know-who put all sorts of killing chemicals in the ground."

She shook her head, looking scandalized. Shawn laughed and caught her in his arms. He liked this whole idea of farming. Since the pack had moved to Devil Mountain, he and Adrian had been working as seasonal hands with the farmers of Deville. They'd built a strong reputation as hardworking and trustworthy guys. That could only help moving forward, and he liked the idea of working for themselves rather than other people.

"Aren't there chemicals in everything?" he teased her.

Jamie lightly slapped his chest but didn't pull away. "I said *killing* chemicals. There is a huge difference between the chemical makeup of a carrot and the chemical makeup of something specifically designed to kill something."

"Ah, I see." Shawn nodded. "Like the chemicals in teeth."

There was a knock on the door and Jamie started squealing. She extracted herself from her mates and bounced over to fling open the door. Lucy, Beth and Jessica stood on the other side. They exchanged hugs and greetings and Jamie ushered them inside. Beth blushed at seeing the two of them, and Jessica scowled slightly. Lucy nodded toward them. She was still looking fairly tired from her ordeal, but from what Shawn had heard, she was doing alright. There didn't seem to be any lasting side-effects of the vampire trying to steal her body.

"Ooh, this looks delicious," Jamie gushed as she took the bottle of wine that Beth offered her. "You're the first to arrive, so go ahead and make yourselves comfortable. I'll just put the mini quiches in the oven. Living room is in there."

Lucy cleared her throat. "Actually, I was just dropping off Jessica and Beth. I don't really feel like book club tonight."

"Are you sure?" Jamie's face fell. "It's my first time hosting in forever. I mean, if you don't want to stay that's fine, but it's less book club tonight and more let's all talk about what's new in our lives."

Lucy hesitated. "Well…"

Adrian cleared his throat. "Sorry to miss Jamie's puppy-dog eyes as she convinces you to stay," he said as he winked at Jamie, who scowled adorably at him, "but Shawn and I are taking off and letting you ladies take care of your evening. So, if you'll—"

"Actually, we wanted to talk to you," Jessica blurted. Her cheeks went red as she glanced at Beth. "There are some papers that we need you to sign, for the Paranormal Marriage Agency. You see… we actually paid out of pocket to get here. And we don't have the funds to leave again. The Agency was supposed to reimburse us, but… since you two didn't technically order us, they're saying that we aren't owed anything."

Shawn frowned. He hadn't ever heard of the marriage agency making their mail-order brides pay their own way. Wasn't that the point of mail-order? That their trips were paid for by other people? "That's rather sloppy of them. You can bring the papers by any time. Glad to help you get back to your own lives."

Both of them looked a little disappointed, as though they had been hoping for something else. Could they…? Shawn scowled. They weren't hoping that they'd leave Jamie for them, were they? Or did they think that because their relationship had two men and only one woman, they needed a side piece to be satisfied!

"We were expecting to be married to shifters," Jessica pressed.

"And we're sorry that you were disappointed," Adrian said.

His tone was cold, and Shawn nodded his approval. It was

one thing for Jessica to imply anything at all, but Jamie was standing right there! They weren't going to stand for that disrespect in their own home. Especially not when she had had to deal with so much disrespect within these walls before. She might have a strong connection to the land and house, but it was going to take work to erase her stepfather's presence from it.

Beth looked properly ashamed. "I don't mind it, really. I absolutely adore little Tanya. I think I'm giving up the marriage agency. I mean, I would like my money back, but I wouldn't want to put you through any trouble."

"You can bring the papers by," Shawn repeated. "Now, I'm sure that you ladies have a wonderful evening planned. So if you'll excuse us—"

"Wait," Jessica blurted. Her gaze flickered to Jamie and she chewed her lip. "Is that how it really works? Two men and one woman? I'm sorry, I know that I don't have any right to say this but—"

"You're right," Lucy snapped suddenly. She glared at Jessica. "I already told you that it's common for wolves. Don't you realize what this looks like?"

Jessica looked abashed and lowered her head. Shawn scowled at her a moment before nodding toward Lucy in appreciation. Jamie was blushing beside her, but she drew herself up quickly enough. "I know it's kind of weird to outsiders," she told Jessica. "But I can assure you that we're all very happy about the situation. Now, maybe you can help me get the mini quiches going?"

Shawn relaxed. That was so much like Jamie. Forgiving Jessica, giving her the benefit of the doubt. Shawn himself would not be so willing to let bygones be bygones—but then, he supposed he was lucky that Jamie was willing to give a person a second chance. Certainly, the way he had acted for the first while when they had known each other left something to be desired.

"We'll be going, then," Adrian said, his tone still cold. "If you need anything, Jamie—"

"I'm sure it will all be fine," Jamie said, waving her hand. "You two go and have fun with the guys. I heard that Jacob and William have a pool table."

"They do," Beth gushed, bouncing on her toes. "Tanya is teaching me how to play."

Shawn and Adrian started for the door but stopped when Jessica made a squeaking noise again. Both stopped to look at her and she gazed back at them with a face flushed red with embarrassment. She took a deep breath as she wrung her hands together. "I'm sorry. I didn't mean to be... like that. I didn't mean to imply anything. About any of you." She glanced at Jamie, looking so miserable that Shawn had to feel sorry for her. "I guess I'm just sort of confused right now. But that was inappropriate and rude of me."

"It was," Adrian agreed before Shawn could brush it off. "But thank you for your apology."

Shawn considered her for a minute. She really was a pathetic sight, standing there all miserable. He glanced at Jamie, who nodded as though she understood what was on his mind. Which wouldn't surprise him at all. He smiled softly at her before focusing on Jessica again.

"Since Adrian and I are moving into this place with Jamie, you can have my cabin," he told her. "That is, if you want your own place. It's big enough, and if you get someone to sublet the hobbit hole you'd be able to pull in some extra money. I'd just ask that you pay utilities. I mean, you did come out here under mistaken pretenses."

Jessica licked her lips then nodded. "Thank you. I'll consider it."

Shawn nodded at her and headed out with Adrian. They hadn't even gotten to the truck, though, when Jamie caught up with them. She threw herself into Shawn's arms and gave him the kind of kiss that made him wish she could just cancel book club and they could have themselves a little bit of fun. He wrapped his arms around her, moaning into her mouth.

"Now, now," Jamie chided as she pulled away. "None of

that. I just wanted to thank you."

"It's more than she deserves after the way she was talking," Adrian grumbled but softened at Jamie's scowl. "But you're right. We don't know what her story is."

"Exactly." Jamie reached for him as well and pulled them both together, holding them tightly. "And thank you. For getting me this farm back. What did you say to him to convince him to leave?"

It had been a surprise to Jamie when her stepfather showed up on their doorstep, handing over the title to the land and saying he was leaving Deville for good. Shawn had been surprised as well, considering there wasn't a mark on him. Obviously, the man was more cowardly than he gave him credit for.

"I just told him that I wasn't going to stand for the way he treated you," Adrian said with a shrug, his cheeks turning pink. "And I might have broken his punching bag. But really, with the way everyone talks about him, I'm surprised he stuck it out this long."

Jamie gave him an appraising look, but her lips curved into a smile. She kissed them both again. "You know, I wanted to leave Deville and the way everyone treated me for so long. If I could have picked up the land and put it somewhere else, I'd have done it in a heartbeat. But who cares what they think, anyway? And as happy as I am that we have this farm, I want you to know that I don't have to stay here. Home is where you guys are."

Shawn drew her closer and pressed a soft kiss to her lips. "I completely agree," he murmured. "And you'll never be homeless again, Jamie. Never."

EPILOGUE

Jamie smacked her lips as she finished off a mini quiche. These things were her favorite food in the entire world. They were so good it was obscene! She licked her lips and reached for another one while beside her Lucy laughed and shook her head.

"They're good are they?"

"Yeah." Jamie grinned as she selected a variety of delicious egg in tiny pastry buckets. "And my wolf likes them, too, so... you know... No reason to deny ourselves."

Lucy laughed again. "So you and your wolf are on better terms now? No more blockers?"

Jamie shrugged, suddenly self-conscious. In her chest her wolf wagged its tail cautiously. It wasn't as though they were this unified team. All the years of trying to deny that her wolf existed combined with the years she spent on blockers, pushing her wolf out of existence entirely, had had an effect. It wasn't something that could just be healed overnight.

"Adrian and Shawn are helping," she said slowly. "They're teaching me how to understand and communicate with it. So yeah, we are on better terms. I guess neither of us is scared of the other one so much. It's hard some days, but

I'm confident that we're going to be okay."
"Good."
"How is yours?" Jamie asked. It was something she had been thinking of. Since the vampire spirit had ripped her in two, literally, it had to have some effects. "You don't have to tell me. I know that you have gone through a lot."
Lucy shook her head. "I'm fine. Or I will be."
Her tone made it clear that she didn't want to continue this conversation. Jamie winced and quickly directed it away. "Now that I'm spending more time with my wolf and indulging it rather than fighting it, I'm starting to realize that it knows what's happening a lot better than I do. Life would have been different if I had trusted it more. Actually, these days I can't even remember why I spent so long denying it."
"Societal pressure is strong, especially in a small town like this." Lucy filled her cup with water and turned her gaze over to Jessica and Beth, who were talking to Chloe, Angela and Miriam. "That might be why those two are so desperate to get married and can't think of having a life without a man in it."
"Maybe," Jamie agreed. "But at the same time, it's not fun to be alone."
Lucy shrugged.
Jessica caught the two of them looking at her and winced. She excused herself from the group and headed over to them. Jamie tensed as her wolf snorted in irritation. Jessica was not exactly the person she wanted to spend a lot of time with, not after the way she had reacted to Adrian and Shawn once more telling her that they weren't interested.
"I wanted to apologize again," Jessica blurted, wringing her hands. "I shouldn't have said that. I didn't mean for it to sound the way it did."
Jamie sighed. "I understand that. You don't have to keep apologizing; it's fine."
And it was. She might be irritated with Jessica, but that didn't mean she was going to be forever angry with her.

She just needed a little more time.

Wanda and Sandra came through the door, calling out their apologies for being late. Both of them looked flushed and excited. Wanda immediately grabbed Jamie into a hug and grinned broadly as she headed for the refreshment table. Apparently her days of trying to strictly diet were over.

"Wanda!" Beth squealed as she flew across the room to hug her. "How are you doing?"

"Not bad," Wanda replied. "My doctor's appointment today was good. Apparently, I have a bit of blockage in my fallopian tubes that's preventing me from ovulating properly. But it's going to be an easy fix; the tests show it's not a severe case. We're hopeful that once it's resolved, the rest will take care of itself."

Miriam nodded as she rounded the refreshment table. "Actually, it's not uncommon. It's the leading cause of infertility among women. Any idea what caused it?"

Wanda shrugged. "I mean, it really could be anything. But since my cycle only started messing up after the whole dragon incident, I think it has something to do with that."

Here, Lucy flinched and stepped back from the group. Nobody seemed to notice, but Jamie did. She reached out, squeezing Lucy's hand gently. It couldn't be easy for her, any of this. She had been a slave to the dragon, too, and the attack on Wanda and Jamie had not been her choice. Lucy, however, faced excruciating pain to help them escape. Nobody blamed her for her actions. Not when she had little choice in the matter.

"Well, we're also looking into adoption," Wanda continued. "After all, we don't know exactly how things are going to go with this. I mean, we're hopeful that I can get pregnant, but we want to explore other options, too. So we're going to get that going and, hopefully, one way or another, we'll end up as parents soon."

"You are so brave," Beth sighed. "I could never adopt."

Miriam and Wanda both gave her puzzled glances. "Why

not?"

"It's just..." Beth ducked her head and blushed. "I know that it doesn't sound good, but I have just... always felt like I couldn't love a child that wasn't mine, you know? I mean, there is something about being pregnant and then giving birth... it's just something that I've always wanted. When I get married, I don't want to wait. I want to have a baby right away. I just don't know if a child can really love someone who isn't their biological mother."

Miriam frowned at her. "Pregnancy and giving birth are not necessary for love or to be a parent, Beth. That's a pretty poor outlook that you have if you think that love is tied to DNA. It's how you treat that child and how you love them, not where they were incubated."

Beth flushed deeper. "I'm just saying. I mean, my father remarried after he divorced my mother, and I was young enough that I don't remember my real mother. Just my stepmother. And she never was a real mother to me."

Here, Jamie frowned. She thought about bringing up her stepfather. He never treated her like a real daughter. She recognized that now looking back. He was the only father figure she'd known in her life, but she wasn't his daughter. And that hurt knowing how much she did love him, but that he didn't love her back. Even though she was still angry and still hated him and had decided that he wasn't worth her time. She was never going to reach out to him again and hopefully one day would never think about him again.

But that wasn't because he wasn't her biological father. That was because he was a pervert, an ass and he should never have been around her to begin with.

Jamie sighed. "The women who give birth to us mess up, too, you know. What happened to your biological mother, if you stepmother wasn't a real mom?"

"I don't know," Beth mumbled, ducking her head. "I went looking for her, but I never could find her."

Jessica rubbed Beth's back, looking defensive as she

glanced around at the others. "Well I don't know about it being impossible for kids not to love stepparents or adoptive parents like their real parents, but I do think it takes someone special to want to adopt. I can't imagine what it would feel like if I had a child who someone might show up one day and try to take back. And I can't imagine how hard it must be for those mothers, giving up their children like that."

"I agree with you there." Jamie nodded. "There needs to be more resources available for people who want to keep their children but feel like they can't because of financial or other reasons. It's sad. So many loving people out there giving up their children for a better life…"

"And so many other children left with people who don't really want them," Sandra agreed. She had a peculiar expression on her face. "You know, Beth, my biological mother raised me. She taught me, fed me, clothed me. She even loved me, in her own way. But she wasn't a good mother. She was abusive, controlling and she stole from me all the time. I'd have taken an adoptive mother who actually cared and took care of me the way a parent ought to over her any day."

Angela nodded. "And Miriam's nephews love her just as much as a child can love any parent. Brian is more of a fostering situation, but he loves Chloe, too."

"His mother basically threw him away," Chloe added. Fury sparked in her eyes as she shook her head. "That woman didn't deserve to call herself his mother! He was in pain and hurting and she walked away as though he wasn't her responsibility."

"So what we're saying," Jamie added as Beth blushed deeper, "is that maybe it wasn't that you didn't love your stepmother as a real mother and more along the lines of she wasn't a real mother at all."

"Sorry," Beth murmured. She ducked her head and twisted her long hair between her fingers, a miserable look coming over her face. "You're right. I didn't mean to say that it was *impossible*. Just that I couldn't do it. Sometimes it really feels like there is something wrong with me. Sometimes I wonder if maybe the universe knows I'd be a terrible mother and that's why I…"

Jamie sighed as she put an arm around Beth. She knew the feeling of wondering if something was wrong with her. "Sometimes we feel broken when it's not our fault, Beth. And as for the universe conspiring against you, I very much doubt that's the case. If women who actively don't want children and punish their children for being born still end up with children, why would someone who wants kids be denied? The universe doesn't care about that sort of thing."

"Besides," Lucy added quietly, "you are good with kids. Tanya adores you, and she's really thriving since you started being her nanny. She's been through a lot in her life, and you have been amazing for her. So maybe you need to open up your way of looking at life a little more. And maybe trust in your own capacity to love more."

Beth flushed a dark red. "Thanks. And I'm sorry. I think maybe it's more of my hang-ups coming forward. It's hard to say sometimes."

"That said," Miriam added as a sly smile crossed her face. "I do think that Wanda is making a brave choice. Not because adoption means anything about not being a real mother—"

"That's not what I said," Beth protested. "I said it was hard for kids to love them as real parents. Not that the parents wouldn't love them."

"Alright," Miriam said, nodding. "But what I was saying was that there is a societal push against adoption. That it's somehow a lesser form of parenting. So it is brave for Wanda to pursue that course as well as looking for treatment to get pregnant."

Jamie nodded and raised her glass. "May the pack ever increase with more children year by year."

"Speaking of, do you have any plans for kids, Jamie?"

Wanda smirked at her as Jamie went beet red.

"Not yet," Jamie mumbled. "We want kids, but we'll be waiting a couple of years to get this place on its feet and then talk about it again. I mean, unless something unexpected happens, of course. But no immediate plans for the pitter-patter of little feet."

"What about you?" Beth turned to Lucy. "Are you...?"

Lucy shook her head. "Not looking for a boyfriend in my life at this time. Maybe a girlfriend. Maybe just being happy being single. My boys will all have to have mates before I even think of adding yet another man into my life." She shook her head again, a long-suffering expression on her face.

"You mean Clinton and Trevor, right?" Beth pressed, her brow furrowing. "Because Jacob and William are married."

Jamie nearly choked on her glass of water. *"What?"*

Her surprise was echoed by most of the other women. Jacob and William had given no indication that they were a couple, rather than the bonded pair that Adrian and Shawn or any of the other women's mates were. Of course that didn't mean that it wasn't there, but it was still a shock to her. They'd had a mate in the past, hadn't they?

Lucy sighed. "Yes, they're married, but it's for legal reasons. There are some instances of shifters in their situation having their children taken from them by the mate's families if their mate dies. They never did get along with Tanya's mother's family. They wanted to make sure that things were solid, so that Tanya couldn't be taken away for any reason. But they don't have that sort of relationship with each other."

"Oh?" Beth pressed, looking a little more interested than was perhaps normal. Jamie smirked. She was bad at hiding her interest.

"When Tanya's mother died they ended up angry. I don't think they've healed from that. Not that they really have had the choice," Lucy added sighing once more. "I would like to see them happy again. Trevor and Clinton, too, but

Jacob and William especially. I hate seeing them so miserable."

Jamie prodded Beth in the ribs. "See? You have a chance at that."

Beth's eyes went wide. "Oh, no! Not me. I couldn't."

"Why?" Miriam frowned at her. "Because that means you'd be Tanya's stepmother?"

"No! No, it's not that at all," Beth protested. "It's just that it's... well, it would be too complicated for me. I signed up for the Paranormal Marriage Agency because I wanted someone who I could utterly devote myself to, who would love me... and if they already had a mate, then that means that was their one shot, wasn't it? Anybody else wouldn't be the same."

"Not being the same doesn't mean that they'd care any less strongly for you," Lucy said gentle. "But I do understand what you mean. It is hard when they already had their fated mate. I wasn't trying to say that you have to pursue them, though. I hope you know that."

"Yes, I understand."

Jamie returned to the table for more mini quiches. It was clear that Beth was interested in Jacob and William. Why else would she look so eager for more information on them? But this sort of thing was tricky; she understood that part.

And, she thought musingly, *if people had been pushing me to be with Shawn and Adrian I would have dug my heels in pretty hard. People don't like to be told what to do.*

All the same, she did hope that Beth would give Jacob and William a chance if they wanted it. It wasn't easy to find someone to hold and love. Having so many people in the mix would only make it more complicated. Besides, she knew that Jacob and William's top priority was Tanya, and they would never make a move unless they thought she would benefit from it. And Lucy was right, Tanya had improved dramatically since Beth had started nannying her. She was getting better at school and was even making friends with some of the kids outside of the pack.

"Well." Beth sighed as she shook her head. "I have a hard time wrapping my head around the polyamory. I know that it's common in shifters and all of you seem to be just fine with it but two guys? I don't how you keep up! Isn't there a lot of chafing?"

The mated women all laughed. Jamie patted Beth's shoulder. "Well, there can be. But the thing is, it's actually pretty amazing. And you figure out ways to make sure everyone is satisfied."

Her mind drifted to the multiple silicone dolls that she and her mates had tucked away. Sometimes the things they did made her shake her head. If she had known about this sort of thing just a year ago, she would have been utterly shocked. But there was a lot of fun to be had in that sort of adventure and exploration. She would have recommended it to Beth, but Beth had that expression on her face like she didn't quite believe her. And really, talking about sex and her sex life was not something Jamie wanted to do in a group, not even her book club!

"Well, I suppose it's just one of those things that I don't understand," Beth said doubtfully. She poured herself some wine as the conversation turned to other things.

Jamie, however, noticed that Beth remained standing there, her gaze distant while everyone else chatted. And she couldn't help but think that she was more interested in all of this than she was letting on. Jessica retreated into herself as well, but her expression wasn't so dreamy. Worry furrowed her brow, but when she met Jamie's eye, it smoothed and she turned to Lucy, drawing her into conversation about what sort of girlfriend she was looking for if she wasn't interested in a boyfriend at the moment.

Jamie sipped her water as she looked around at her friends, gathering in her own house for the first time. It wasn't going to be the last time, either. A smile spread over her face. Her home. Her friends. And waiting for her at the end of the night? Her mates.

Life, she decided, might be hard. It might be rough, and it might drive you crazy at times. But if you could just hold on through the dark times, there was always a brighter dawn waiting for you.

*****

THE END

THANK YOU

Thank you so much for reading "Promised to the Wolves"!

Hopefully, you enjoyed reading my book as much as I did writing.

I would appreciate if you'd be willing to share a review that allows me to continuously improve my books and motivates me to keep writing.

Also a big thank you to my husband and my son. Your support means the world to me!

P.S. Stay tuned, there are more books in the "Devil Mountain Wolf Shifters" series to follow:

Kidnapped by the Wolves (Book 1)
Sold to the Wolves (Book 2)
Surrogate to the Wolves (Book 3)
Enslaved by the Wolves (Book 4)
Seduced by the Wolves (Book 5)
Promised to the Wolves (Book 6)
Bitten by the Wolves (Book 7)
Hunted by the Wolves (Book 8)

ABOUT THE AUTHOR

Jasmine Wylder is a Real Estate Agent by day and an emerging Paranormal Romance Author & Adventurer by night. Hailing from California, her passion for sultry stories, steamy scenes, and all-things romance began early on and it has stayed with her ever since.
When she isn't creating captivating storylines, Jasmine loves spending time in the great outdoors, practicing yoga, and treating herself to fine cuisine.
Whether it's out-of-this-world love (literally), dragon shifters setting your heart ablaze, or unquenchable vampiric desire, Jasmine has you covered!

Want more of Jasmine Wylder? Stay social with her:

Join her Reader's Group on Facebook:
http://bit.ly/JWylder

Like her publisher's Facebook Fan Page:
https://www.facebook.com/PurePassionReads/

Follow her on BookBub:
https://www.bookbub.com/profile/jasmine-wylder

Follow her on Amazon:
http://author.to/JasmineWylder

Printed in Great Britain
by Amazon